All The Way By Water
A Historical Novel

A pioneer family's travels by flatboat on the Ohio and Mississippi Rivers

Byron Grush

Published in the United States by Broadhorn Publishing, Delavan, Wisconsin.

ISBN-10: 0615720714
ISBN-13: 978-0615720715 (Broadhorn Publishing)

Cover illustration, "Tower-Rock, Ansicht vom Missisippi," aquatint by Karl Bodmer, from *Maximilian, Prince of Wied's Travels in the Interior of North America* by Bodmer completed during the years 1832–1834

To my children, their children, their children's children and the many future generations to come—and to the pioneering spirit they shall inherit, coupled with a tolerance and understanding of other people.

ACKNOWLEDGMENTS

I couldn't have persevered on this project without the support (and spell checking) of my wife, Martha. She put up with my obsession with genealogy and my passion for historical trivia, dutifully reading each chapter and trying in vain to make me understand certain grammatical nuances that escaped me. My sister, Mary, who spent many hours staring at computer screens, finding obscure notations of family history and sharing these with me, and lending a hand with the editing, was indispensable in researching the family history and finalizing the manuscript. Also I would like to thank Nancy Mego who, beyond the call of duty, gave the book another once over and offered many suggestions.

I should also mention my father, who, when he was alive, instilled in me an interest in the "archeology" of searching for graveyards and homesteads, an interest that lay dormant in me for many years, and my mother, who instilled in me a love of writing and taught me everything I know about it.

The curator of the Polo History Museum, Betty Obendorf, kindly and skillfully extracted obituaries of my Great Great Grandfather and my Great Grandfather from their archives, which aided me tremendously. Roger Cramer, historian of Ogle County, Illinois, and creator of a genealogical web site, communicated with me to trade historical Grush family data. And finally, David Dahl, current owner of what was the John B. Grush farm, was kind enough to share what he knew about the house and the barn which still stands in Pine Creek Township.

CHAPTER 1
STANDING STONE

Huntingdon County, Pennsylvania. 23 May, 1845

Isaac Grosh ran his hands along the rough surface of the limestone pillar, his fingers tracing the incised markings of the names and dates of early settlers to the Juniata River Valley. Twice as tall as a man and the width of a railroad tie, the monument known as Standing Stone stood on the very spot where Iroquois had once erected a similar pillar, a totem, covered with sacred petroglyphs. Now this new pillar acknowledged the deeds of brave white men, some of whom had driven the Indians out of their native lands.

"1744 Jack Armstrong kilt on Jack's Mt by savages," read one inscription. "Col. Croghan 1760, Founder," read another. Isaac recognized many names from stories he had heard in his youth. Here was "1767 Rev Dr Wm Smith," who had named the small village Huntingdon after an English countess. There was "1774 Bartholomew Davis," who built the first grist mill at Shirleysburg. And "1777 Capt Wm McAlevy," commander of a company that fought for independence against British forces in the Revolutionary War.

These were men and woman of courage, Isaac knew: adventurous, risking their very lives to open up the wilderness for commerce, for freedom and independence. Isaac always stopped here at Standing Stone on his trips to Huntingdon to make deliveries and buy supplies. He would muse about these pioneers, their hardships and the rewards that came for their perseverance in the face of peril. To taste of the purity of virgin territory! To walk under the canopy of old growth timber, along the crystal waters of streams and rivers untouched by industry. To hunt and fish as the Tuscarora Indians had, with trap and bow, net and line. Isaac's eyes seemed glazed as he became engulfed in reverie for a nostalgia he could not own.

Isaac wore the long coat and wide-brimmed hat like those of the German peasant class of old that members of the Brethren Church adopted for their act of "living plain." He had a long beard that accented the length of his face. In November, Isaac would turn 48. He had resided in German Valley near Shirleysburg, some 20 miles away, for nearly 30 years and raised four sons and four daughters. Enough life for any man. But the blood of noble Huguenots flowed in his veins. Ancestors who fled from religious persecution in France to Germany, then ventured forth to the new world of America—this was the source of the fearless pioneering spirit that lay dormant in Isaac. A spirit that refused to slumber quietly. As he walked back to the wagon he nodded to his two eldest sons, Philip and John, who sat erect and proud on the driver's seat.

"I think we'll take the old trail back," Isaac said. "Too much hustle and bustle on the new road."

"It will take a mite longer," said Philip, the older of the two boys, just 19 but already headstrong and not afraid to contradict his father.

"Mother will really like the fabric you bought for her, Pop," said John. A year younger than Philip, John was eager to please his father and often took his cues from Philip, but contrary to his older brother's independency, he never opposed Isaac.

"Came up from Baltimore. Some kind of French cloth they said. It's simple enough, though. Yes, Catherine will like it. Probably make a new dress." Isaac took the reins and clicked his tongue at Sampson, the mule.

The wagon began to creak along Allegheny Street toward the Juniata and Jack's Narrows, where the river broke through Jack's Mountain. From here they would follow the Juniata to Aughwick Creek where they could branch off and take the Aughwick trail back to Shirleysburg. The mountainous Southwestern Pennsylvania terrain was ribbed with ridges and valleys, the river flats being fertile soil for farming and the variety of geological strata offering iron ore and coal in abundance. Many of the old Indian trails ran along creek beds and connected the small communities that had sprung up at the sites of the original white settlements. Old Aughwick, once an Indian village, became the location where Fort Shirley was built to protect settlers from hostile Indians and British Tories. Now the town of Shirleysburg was home to several hundred people: miners, millers, farmers and tradesmen.

Isaac was a cooper by trade, a builder of wooden vessels bound with metal rings. Many a barrel or cask made by him found its way filled with grain or nails, dry goods or gunpowder, to markets as far away as New Orleans, traveling by boat along canals and the great waterways of the Ohio and Mississippi Rivers. The boys, Philip, John, William and James were apprenticing to Isaac at his shop. William was 15 and perhaps the most enthusiastic learner of the four. He was developing a more than adequate skill at shaping the wooden staves to the correct curvatures. James, though, being at the awkward age of 13 and still in school, didn't share the interest or work ethic of his siblings.

As the wagon clattered along, turkey vultures glided in ever descending spirals in the sky above. Something had died and was now part of the endless cycle of life, its bowels and flesh giving sustenance to roving vermin and scavengers eager to pick clean its bones. In the distance they saw a thickening haze collecting across Blue Ridge, proclaiming a diminishing day. They could smell a faint odor of smoldering charcoal in the wind that wafted over the creek and rustled the low branches of the dogwood and redbud trees. Sampson dutifully kept a steady pace as the wagon rumbled over gravel and sand, hardened into something like a road by a century of travel. The fly net thrown across the mule's back had a long fringe which swung and undulated like the costume of a Middle Eastern dancer.

The boys were husky, agile young men who sometimes exhibited more energy than mindful prudence. John, though younger, was taller than his brother by a few inches which may have piqued Philip at times. John looked up to Philip but was hesitant to admit it. A friendly rivalry played out in both physical and verbal taunts between the two but their loyalty to each other was resolute. Indeed, Philip had saved John from drowning one summer when they were six and five years of age. As they played along the side of the river, John claimed he could jump across to the other bank. Philip, of course, provided the necessary dare and John proceeded to back off some little distance to prepare for a dash. The river at this point was not deep nor exceptionally wide, but the current was swift and the boulders lining the river bottom were sharp-edged.

"Better not try it," called Philip. But this enlivened John as no jeer or mockery could have done.

"Watch this," shouted John and he ran toward the river, leaping high above the raging torrent. But his jump was short and he landed with a great splash in the middle of the Juniata. At first, Philip laughed the laugh of a brother vindicated by John's foolishness and hence, his own superiority. John, however, did not rise, soaking and sputtering in defeat, his own good-natured laugh adding to the hilarity. He lay still as the water tugged and turned him, and he began to be carried down stream. Without hesitating, Philip dove into the Juniata, and pulled John to safety. A great deal of water exited from John's mouth as he revived. The boys never spoke of the incident afterwards.

Now Philip and John nudged and jostled each other on the wagon's bench, playing at, to Isaac's thinking, the foolish games of unruly children. He gave them the stern look he had used to quell such activities when they were much younger, but it was to no avail. Could these young men carry on tradition as responsible adults when they exhibited such antics? Then he remembered a time when he had been John's age and his own father had uprooted the family to move westward across the state to this valley. He had acted the fool more than once, teasing his younger sister and wrestling with his brothers when he should have been helping his father with the new farmstead. He was neither punished nor shamed by either of his parents, but he soon came to realize his idleness was a burden to them.

"Isaac, I want you to feed and water the hogs," said his father one summer morning. "Be sure they get water. That sow is on the verge of giving birth and I don't want her dehydrated."

Isaac had heard his father's instructions, but somehow, the lure of a fishing pole and the cool rush of creek water called with a greater persuasion. He would do his chores when he returned. Later that afternoon, Isaac wandered back to the farm, pole over shoulder and bucket of river trout in hand. He stopped short when he recognized Mr. Sorensen's buggy on the road. Mr. Sorensen was an animal doctor. Something was wrong. The sow had miscarried and bled out. There would be no new piglets this season. And the sow? Good only for bacon and ham now. He saw the look of disappointment on his father's face and it shook him. It was a simple thing, a subtle warning that heralded a sudden awareness of his place in the world. A turning point that would cement an ethic he now wished to impart to his sons. But how?

"Boys," said Isaac, "I want you two to do the deliveries yourselves this summer."

"You mean you trust us?" asked Philip.

"I trust you will stay out of that Irishman's tavern. You meet the wrong kind of women there. You will deliver barrels to Johnson's and come directly home."

"But Pop," said John, "where will you be?"

"I want to give your grandpa some help out on the farm. He can't afford the hands anymore and, frankly, I'm pretty interested in farming these days."

"You really love that old man, don't you, Pop?"

"Yes, I do, John. And you two could learn a great deal from him."

"Should we be helping too? I'm good with animals."

"I want you and Philip to work the cooperage. You've learned a lot about the trade. You will have to make a decision soon, and the more experience you have, the better you will choose."

"Choose? What do we need to choose?"

"Yes," said Philip. "What ever are you talking about? Decisions? Are you leaving the shop? Is that it? You want us to take it over while you go help out Grandpa?"

"Something along those lines, Philip."

"Have you discussed this with Mom?"

"Your mother, bless her, always goes along with my wishes. But there is more to it than that. I'll tell you all about it as soon as I get some things worked out. For now, just do your work and think about what you want from life."

Isaac handed the reins to Philip and settled back. He shut his eyes, perhaps to stop the wetness from showing, or perhaps just to rest. He drifted into a light sleep as the wagon rocked and the rhythm of Sampson's hoofs sang out against the gravel. In a dream, he saw his name emblazoned on the Standing Stone.

CHAPTER 2
GERMAN VALLEY

Near Shirleysburg, PA, 23 May, 1845

It was late evening when they arrived at the house. Catherine heated up the stew in a large iron kettle while Philip and John saw to Sampson, wiping him down and securing him in the stable. Will and James were playing checkers by the light of an oil lamp and the girls, being younger, had already retired for the night. Isaac kissed his wife softly on the back of the neck as she stood stirring stew at the cast iron wood burning stove.

"Another long day, Husband?"

"A very long day, Catherine. They seem to get longer and longer."

Isaac and Catherine had built the frame house on his father's farm land with the help of neighbors living in the German Valley community. Many had come here from Lancaster County in the eastern part of the state where their German and Dutch ancestors had immigrated nearly a century ago. Many were members of the Moravian Church and called themselves "The Brethren." Brethren prospered in the freedom of the new world and formed agrarian settlements seeped in religious belief and communal spirit. The Brethren in German Valley were at the ready when a new barn or a house needed erecting. The wood was hewn from local ash and white oak, now rapidly diminishing in abundance. There were real glazed windows and a fireplace. Two bedrooms occupied the second story, one for the girls and one for the boys. Downstairs was a kitchen with an eating area, a sitting room, and a third bedroom where Isaac and Catherine did their own communing.

Catherine had been born in Huntingdon County. When

she married Isaac, she was nineteen years of age, he was twenty-three. After a year, twins were born to the young couple. They named them Philip and Isaac. Catherine took to motherhood well and pampered the twins, keeping them warm and secure during an unusually cold winter. A crazy quilt made by her maternal grandmother covered them in their crib as Catherine sang them sweet lullabies. By early spring Baby Isaac had developed a cold, a running nose and a slight cough. When she felt his forehead he was burning with fever. The cough worsened, becoming a wheezing fitful seizure lasting several minutes, during which the baby's color shifted from pink to red to purple. This subsided for a time and Isaac seemed to recover, only to be struck again with severe coughing. A week later, the infant was dead. Catherine was devastated.

Her father, a wheelwright, made a small pine coffin; its craftsmanship was impeccable. On a cold January morning they stood on the hill of the Brethren Cemetery, surrounded by friends and family as the tiny wooden box was lowered into the frozen ground. Isaac took Catherine's hand in his own, stifled a gasp, and turned his eyes toward heaven in a silent prayer. "Oh Lord," he said, "never take this woman from me!" It was this sad misfortune, this *tod von kindern*, this death of children, which had welded them forever emotionally and spiritually inseparable. Isaac had admired Catherine's delicate features, particularly those dark brown eyes of hers. She had a capricious, almost quirky expression, drawn perfectly upon alabastine skin that had enchanted him from the beginning. Catherine had been attracted to Isaac's stately demeanor, his nearly gaunt but authoritative stature with its air of silent, secretive power. Their young love might have been fleeting, might have degenerated into familiar regard and pleasant companionship. Then, with the death of their child, Isaac questioned his wisdom in joining with another, only to share grief and disaster. And Catherine too had doubts. What had she brought upon this kind, strong man—what would she bring to the future?

But within that single moment when their hands sought each other's, when the tears and wailing ceased, it was as if the gray sky had brightened and the frigid snow had faded away. They knew they had endured the worst that could come to them and their bond was strengthened by the realization. The real marriage began on that day, not needing the sanction of religion or family, not needing discussion or rationalization, not needing a pledge or a paper. It simply came into being in the way in which the wind picks up a leaf and spirals it endlessly aloft.

"You shouldn't work so hard, Isaac," Catherine said as she placed a hot plate of stew on the table in front of her husband. Philip and John joined their father and began gobbling glistening vegetables and chunks of beef with the gusto of very hungry men. Isaac poked at his food tentatively, rolling a potato over in the thick gravy. This didn't escape Catherine's notice.

"Not so hungry, Dear?"

"It's not the stew, Cat, I'm just thinking on some things." Catherine knew that when Isaac called her by the endearment, "Cat," that something serious was afoot.

"Pop wants Philip and me to run the shop," piped in John, eliciting one of Isaac's stern glances.

"What's that?" said Will, nearly upsetting the checker board as he rose to his feet.

"I just think it's time for Philip and John to take on more responsibility, that's all," explained Isaac.

"They're gonna be my boss?" asked Will, joining the family at the table.

"Children," admonished Catherine, "should be seen and not heard!" William was her favorite, if it could be said that she had a favorite among the boys, and thus she tended to reprimand him more harshly than the others when such an occasion arose. This compensated for the extra love and adoration she felt for William in a special way that mothers understand, but boys do not.

Nor do fathers, for Isaac took William's concern to heart and turned to him, saying, "You are just as important, Will. Philip and John are a little older, and will have to make deliveries and take orders. You are a fine craftsman and will be in charge of overseeing all the building of vessels— keeping the quality in line with our reputation."

"What about me?" yelled James from the corner of the room.

"You," said Catherine, "are going to get ready for bed. We'll talk about all this in the morning!" And that was the final word as the boys finished their dinner in silence and Isaac and Catherine looked at each other with the mutual understanding that, in fact, there hadn't actually been a final word.

The next morning, the family awakened just as the reddening sky announced the eminent rising of the sun. Breakfast was fresh buttered bread, sizzling slabs of bacon, and hot coffee for the older boys and their parents. A pot of oatmeal sat in the middle of the table, from which Will and James scooped large portions into their bowls. The girls, having set the table and helped their mother with the cooking, had already nibbled at the bread and slurped down bowls of oatmeal while the men were washing up. Mary Jane, who was eleven, and Elizabeth, who was nine, would be accompanying their brother, James, to the schoolhouse in Shirleysburg. The younger girls, Emma, five, and Catherine, two, would remain home with Mother.

Philip hitched Sampson to the wagon while John and Will loaded the coil of copper banding they had purchased in Huntingdon. Mary Jane and Elizabeth were engaged in a game of Jacks on the covered porch, while James rocked incessantly back and forth on Isaac's favorite rocking chair.

"Hey, Jimmy, come and help!" yelled John.

"Aw, I'm going to school today. Not working," came an answer that challenged John's sense of fairness. But he let it pass, knowing it was useless to spar with his younger brother over trivialities. Although he thought James was a bit of a slacker and arrogant as well, he was fond and protective of him. Perhaps some of Philip's stewardship of John had transferred to John's relationship with James. James would come around eventually, John knew. When he was most needed, James would rally to the cause. Until then, however, he rocked.

James was the adventurous one of the four boys. When he was six he decided he was a Knight of the Round Table and commandeered a neighbor's prize hog as a steed. He took off toward Black Log Mountain with the hog in tow, waving a willow branch that was just the proper length for a broad sword. That same willow branch functioned well when it was later applied to the seat of his pants. At age ten he had coaxed Mary Jane into skinny dipping in Aughwick Creek, an infraction which was sufficient for the addition of another notch in the willow branch. The fabled branch leaned against a corner in the house, its several notches a seductive warning and a challenge to the young boy.

"Twosies," called Elizabeth, bouncing the rubber Jack ball in the air and snatching two of the metal, six-pronged "knucklebones" in time to catch the ball. The set of Jacks had been her special Christmas present last year. Before its arrival in their small gaming arsenal they had had to make do with stones and pebbles, or, if available, the tiny bones from a pig's foot. Twosies would be followed by threesies and so forth, until she missed the ball or collected all the "bones." "Allsies," called out Mary Jane, requiring Elizabeth to attempt to collect all of the bones at one try. She threw the ball down with extra force just as the screen door creaked open and Father Isaac appeared in the doorway.
"Time for school, girls," he said. "James! That's my chair you're in. You're rocking too high! Go get into the wagon!"
"Yes sir," replied James, knowing when it was wise to act the good child, even though he would have preferred to rock rigorously right off the edge of the porch, a feat he had only attempted once before, and would have accomplished had not his father appeared prematurely on the scene.
"We're all set to go," called Philip from the wagon.
"Off with you then. You're on your own today. The children will come down to the shop after school and you can bring them home when your work is done."
"Going to visit Grandpa, Pop?" asked John.
"Just pay attention to your own beeswax, John. Have a good day, and we'll see you at dinner."
The sun was beginning to warm the fertile green valley as the wagon rumbled along Germany Valley Road toward Shirleysburg. Sampson fell into his usual spirited canter (if a mule can be said to canter) and the clip-clop-clip beating of his hoofs sounded rhythmic and musical against the creaking and groaning of the old wagon. Mary Jane and Elizabeth giggled together over some secret revelation about school or classmates or just a young girl's happiness at

being alive. James hung over the side of the wagon, watching the road unraveling as they passed the few farms and cottages between the here and the there of the morning's commute. School would be boring: recitation, sums, capitals of the states, names of the presidents. He was too old to still be cooped up with the younger children in that one-room schoolhouse. He couldn't escape the chores that the older children were assigned: carrying water, bringing in wood for the stove in winter, sweeping, and cleaning. At least it was nearly summer!

"Watch your sister for a while," Catherine told Emma. There was a rag doll or two to play with, so the girls were momentarily content. "Sit down with me, Husband. Have another cup of coffee."

"You know, Cat, I've been thinking."

"Yes, Dear?"

"There is some very cheap land for sale in Illinois. The railroad has put it up."

"Illinois?"

"Listen to this letter I got from my nephew last week" Isaac began to read:

Dear Uncle Isaac,

I take this privilege to rite to you that we are able and hope that these few lines may find you in the same state of health. I promised to rite to you as soon as I got to the west but I have neglected it but now I beg your kindness that you will not think hard of it that I did not write to you sooner as after I got to Rock River I had a severe attack of the bilious fever.

"Oh, Isaac, please spare me the details," said Catherine. He smiled, then continued.

Uncle Isaac you should come and move with us to Rock River Settlement. I have got eighty acres of land that I traded the horse and carriage for. I got it for 1.50 cts. per acre. There is many chances yet and first rate Country that a man can make a better liven there then in any Country that I ever was in for they can rais from thirty to fifty bushels to the acre without any expence onely there labour for the land is smooth. I think it is better for at once to leave all and go to Illinois for now is the time to get land cheap for in two years time all the best chances will be taken up for there is many people going to that Rock River Settlement.

"You see, Dear," said Isaac, pausing his narration, "he talks about the quality of the land out there and it's very cheap. The land in Pennsylvania has gotten out of hand—and scarce!"

"But Isaac, Darling, you aren't a farmer. And how would we get there?"

"Let me read more," said Isaac.

I would like to see you and the family come out next summer to Ogle County Illinois that is the place that we are going to. The market was good for to be a new country wheat was seling for seventy five cts per bushel corn twenty cts a bushel when I left that country beef 4 cts per pound pork 5.00 per hundred milch cows from 12 to 15 dollars. I started from Illinois for home on the 20 day of October and landed on the 11 of November. I came home all the way by water.

Your respectful nephew,

Phillip Eby

"Less than a month by water, he says. There are those same flatboats that take goods down to New Orleans that are used to transport whole families. When you reach the big river, you go up instead of down."

"By boat? Isaac, I don't know. I all sounds so... frightening! We have a good living here. The children have their friends. You are bringing Philip and John into the cooperage with you. And your parents are here. My family too. It just seems so impossible."

"Cat, my darling, Cat. Your sister, Amelia and her husband are talking about going. My sister and Phillip Eby will be there. Other families in the church are going. And I intend to let Philip and John make their own decisions about whether to come with us. They will run the cooperage by themselves and can stay and have a good life here if they like."

"Oh, Isaac. What is to become of us?" And that was the final word—for a while.

CHAPTER 3
THE COOPERAGE

Shirleysburg, Pennsylvania, 24 May, 1845

Will selected a piece of white oak from the drying rack where the logs, hand-split and quartered were stacked. He cut this to length then began to pull the shaver along it, tapering it toward the ends and hollowing it slightly in the middle. When he was satisfied with the shape of the stave he placed it inside a metal hoop along side other staves that radiated like the petals of some giant, inverted wooden flower. Once all the staves were in place, he would position the unfinished barrel over a small fire until the insides were charred and the wood became flexible. Then he could use a winch to arch and tighten the staves into the shape of the barrel and secure it with more metal hoops. A croze grove would be cut for the barrel heads and a bung hole bored so that the customer could fill the barrel with wine or beer.

Will's barrel would take him an entire day to make. John started to assemble another "flower" from staves already prepared. That work was slow and required a presence of mind as well as an innate artistry, both of which they had learned from their father. Philip also built barrels, but today he would venture forth to barter for more of the excellent oak with its extra thick rays they were getting from a lumberman up on the Blue Ridge. While the "mise en rose," or raising of the barrel continued, the boys began to talk about the strangeness they had observed in their father.

John postulated that Father Isaac was growing old and tired. Perhaps he was sick, wondered Will. Philip suggested that placing them in charge of the cooperage did not foretell Isaac's retirement, merely that he wished to secure their involvement in the family business, in case they became stricken with wanderlust and strayed from the fold. Was it true that Grandfather needed help on the farm? They didn't think so. Hadn't their father said there was more to it?

"I've heard some rumors about families moving west," said John. "Maybe he wants to make sure we'll all stay at home and not leave him and Mother."

"I should like to see the West," Will said, pounding a stave up tight against the hoop with a wooden mallet.

"I would too," agreed John.

"What would you do if you went there?" asked Philip.

"I'd be a cooper," replied Will. "I can make barrels there as easily as here."

"We could fight Indians," said John. "Are there still any Indians left to fight?"

"Some," said Philip, joining in John's tomfoolery. "You'd need to watch out for your scalp, Will."

"Aw, I'd bring my musket and shoot 'em right between the eyes if they made trouble!"

"You couldn't hit the side of a barn with a twelve pound cannon!" John quipped.

"I could! I'm as good a shot as you any day of the week!"

"Anyway," Philip interjected, "people from here are going to Ohio or Indiana. There are no buffalo there so—no Indians."

"Yes there are. I heard about hostile Indians even living here at Augwick, not so long ago."

"A hundred years, maybe." And so it went while the barrels rose and the fires were lit. Philip left to meet the lumberman up the road where he was bringing a load of wood into town to sell. Will and John continued their repartee while they worked. The conversation meandered from Indians and sharp shooting to a circus which was coming to Huntingdon in August, to whether the wine was real that was served at the church during Love Feast. It was sweetened tea, maintained John. Deacon Bell had a bottle, insisted Will. He and Becky Cornelius had seen him sampling it one Sunday after church.

Shirleysburg, built on the site of Old Fort Shirley, was laid out along the main road in a clearly logical order.

Residences were mostly tucked away on short blocks branching off Croghan Pike, while businesses, like the Grosh Cooperage, Vail's General Store, Harrison's Livery, and the Horse Flynet Factory, were spaced up and down the Pike like buttons on a high top shoe. There were three churches and one school. The white clapboard schoolhouse sported a square shaped cupola in which a bell, made from the melted iron of a Revolutionary War cannon, rang once in the morning to announce the start of class, once at one o'clock to bring the children back from the playground, and a third time at four o'clock, heralding the cessation of the day's instruction.

The playground was a rectangular area of dirt, which often blew up in a high wind to coat the children's faces, sting their eyes and foul their hair. Handfuls could be used as missiles during battle games and many a mud pie was constructed during rainy weather. Two wooden swings dangled from long ropes tied high in the branches of an ancient maple. These were jealously coveted resulting in shouting, pushing, and occasionally in fisticuffs during recess. At least one child lost front teeth from the impact with a swing each year. The tilting boards were painted bright green and the children thought it extraordinarily funny that their teacher, Miss Latta, who was from back east, called it a "teeter-totter." This became the root of myriad jests.

Benjamin Pergrin, the oldest student in the school, was given the job of ringing the four o'clock bell. At the very first dong a shout arose and eighteen children, clutching slates and pencil boxes, rushed for the door. Miss Latta remonstrated, but the clamor remained unchecked. James and his sisters filed out in as disorderly a manner as any of them and headed down the pike. Vail's General store was a waypoint between the school and the cooperage, its array of glass containers filled with penny candy being the main attraction. The children often stopped there on the way home.

Despite two display windows at the front of the store, Vail's was dark, musty, and felt hauntingly mysterious to Mary Jane and Elizabeth. The sagging floor was cluttered with wooden crates and barrels and the walls lined with shelves from floor to ceiling. Dusty bolts of cloth and jars with paper labels, coils of rope and hammers, underwear, crockery, lanterns, colorful boxes of patent medicines and remedies were displayed in a haphazard arrangement that was categorically indecipherable. Elizabeth was drawn to a doll with a porcelain head and painted eyes and mouth that sat along side a cardboard package of suspenders. James was fascinated by a pair of hand guns in a glass case on the counter. Next to that was a coffee grinder, a balance scale, a ledger book and sales pad and an open cash box with dividers for different denominations of bills and coins.

The threesome gazed longingly at jars of candy sticks, peppermints and horehound drops, candied orange peel, molasses taffy pulls, kisses and meringues. Ephraim Vail, the proprietor, appeared suddenly from behind the counter where he had been chasing a small gray mouse with an axe handle.

"And what may I do for you today?" he enquired.

"Three cents worth of horehound drops," replied James.

"No, no! The taffy," cried Elizabeth.

"One taffy, one horehound drop and one meringue," insisted Mary Jane, always the politician.

"Well, I've got the money," complained James.

"One taffy, one horehound and one meringue coming up," said Ephraim Vail, always the arbitrator.

As the candy was exchanged for the three coins, James pointed to the hand guns in the glass case. "May I hold one?" he asked. Ephraim Vail thought about this, not being in the habit of giving fire arms to children. But he recognized James as the son of one of his suppliers and since he never kept fire arms loaded in the store, decided to accommodate the lad. As he reached into the case to withdraw one of the revolvers, he saw, having excellent peripheral vision, that the lad had swiped a few more horehound drops from the jar. But being good natured and remembering having been a mischievous boy himself, Ephraim feigned not seeing the theft. Turning, he placed the gun in the boy's hands and explained:

"This is a Colt Paterson five shot revolver. You see, you cock back this hammer with your thumb and the cylinder turns, moving a bullet into position, then the trigger swings out of the handle there. Then you pull the trigger and you can hit your target at 65 yards if you aim right. Shoot five in a row before you have to reload. The U. S. Army is buying them and so are those Texas people down south. You tell your Paw he might like one of these when he goes out west."

"What? Pop going out west? What did you say?"

"I thought I heard your family was moving west. Maybe I heard wrong."

"I don't know anything about it. Do you, Mary Jane?" Mary Jane shook her head, no. "Liz—?" Elizabeth also indicated negatively. James gingerly handed the revolver back to Mr. Vail. He was momentarily speechless. Could there be something going on in the family that he didn't know about? Suddenly he was in a hurry to get to the cooperage to talk to his older brothers. This certainly was something of monumental importance!

Catherine eased the sleeping two-year-old onto her trundle bed. Finally exhausted after an afternoon of frenzied playing, little Catherine, or Katy as they now called her, had fought off drowsiness through two books and a "make-believe" which had equally exhausted her mother. Emma had entertained her sister for most of the day, creating fantasy games in which she was the Queen and Katy a Lady in Waiting. The unfairness of this arrangement had not occurred to the younger child. She was delighted to have received so much attention from Emma who naturally wanted to play older games by herself. One of Emma's chores was to relieve Catherine for part of the day by minding her sibling, a task she preferred to handle according to her own devices.

Isaac had just returned from his father's farm, tired, and needful of companionship. Emma was sent to fend for herself while Isaac and Catherine sat on the porch, he in his rocker, she in a wicker chair for which she had sewn over-stuffed pillows from cloth decorated with trumpet vines and blooms.

"Am I getting old, Catherine?" he asked.

"Do you feel old, Husband?"

"No... I feel... I feel like I'm getting my second wind."

"Then you're not old, Isaac." Catherine pulled an embroidery hoop from a sewing bag along side of her chair. "You really want to move to Illinois, don't you—?"

"It would be a new life. Hard, there's no denying it. But we'd live off the land! Be independent. Be part of a new, young country. Just think of it!"

"I am thinking of it. I'm thinking of the good school we have here, our friends, the church, our parents and brothers and sisters."

"We'll have all that and more, Catherine. I promise you."

The screen door swung open and Katy burst out, hurtling herself up on her mother's lap and knocking the embroidery hoop to the porch floor.

"Well, that was a short nap!"

"Mama! Not tired!" Catherine drew the girl to her in an embrace that spoke not only to her love for the little girl, but to a grasping for comfort such as when one senses a storm approaching—a storm with lightning and thunder and furious winds.

Later, dinner finished, dishes washed and put up in the cupboard, Isaac called his family back to the table. A family meeting, he said. He and Catherine sat at opposite ends of the long oak table, the boys on one side and the girls on the other. Katy was fidgeting so Catherine brought her again to her lap. Now Emma began to complain. "This concerns you as well," came the reprimand from her father. There were no surprised looks on the boys faces, nor on Mary Jane's nor Elizabeth's, as they had all discussed the prospect of moving earlier when James had arrived at the cooperage to deliver Ephraim Vail's pronouncement of that possibility. It fit their unfinished theories about their father's strange behavior and intrigued them as well as presenting them with a dilemma.

"Next spring," began Isaac, "I plan on moving this family to Illinois where I will buy a farm and we will homestead." There was silence. "I intended to wait to tell you this because I wanted Philip and John to have the chance to remain here if they so desire. They are almost of age and could have a good business to run if they stay in the cooperage."

"Father," said Philip, "we have already talked about this.

We've made our decision. We stay with the family. We will go with you to Illinois."

The flickering flame from the overhead oil lamp reflected in a moistness that was forming in Isaac's eyes. He brushed this away and stiffened. He looked to Catherine, now clutching Katy to her bosom. He read the concern on her features. There would be a long year of preparation, a house and a business to sell, a boat to acquire, goodbyes to orchestrate. He was asking a lot of his family but they would support him in his venture, giving him an even greater reason to succeed. Catherine met his glace, smiled weakly, and nodded.

CHAPTER 4
FATHERS AND SONS

German Valley, Pennsylvania, 25 May, 1845

Philip Grosh, Isaac's father and the man for whom Isaac had named his oldest son, had been born in Earl Township in Lancaster County near Philadelphia during the American Revolutionary War. He had been born as had the new country, through struggle and strife, with pride and forbearance: the progeny of persecution. His father, Christopher, had immigrated to the new world from Germany by way of Holland on a wave of protestant refugees which had begun two hundred years before as the Huguenots fled death and destruction in their native France.

Christopher was witness and participant to another birth, that of the United Brethren Church. He found himself at a crowded meeting in an old barn in the town of Lancaster one evening in 1762. He was moved by the speech given by a Mennonite preacher who, in decrying the rituals and hierarchies of the Church of Rome, urged that common folk cry out to God while tilling the fields. Someone called out, "We are all brethren," and a new church was born. Christopher found in it a calling and aspired to its clergy.

Like father, son Philip was deeply involved in Brethren Church life. After he had moved his family to the German Valley in Huntingdon County, he became a founding member of the Brethren Church there. He raised his own children in the belief that religion must be the experience of daily life—simple and unadorned, achieved through hard work and the sharing of values. From Christopher to Philip the elder, to Isaac, to Philip the younger and the others was passed a sense of duty to family and community. But now it seemed to Philip that the younger generations were drifting away, seeking to strike out on their own. It was difficult to understand.

He stood in the shade of the barn, its weathered wood siding awaiting the white wash he would apply next spring. Perhaps Isaac and his sons would help with the painting. The boys, of course, would suggest decorating the barn with one of those geometric or floral circle patterns called hex signs that were becoming popular. None of that superstitious nonsense for Philip Grosh! Tall and lean, with tanned forearms exposed by the rolled up sleeves of his blue cotton shirt, Philip was the quintessential vision of the Pennsylvania Dutch farmer. His face was clean shaven save for a long beard which hung goat-like from his chin. His dark pants were held up by suspenders and a wide-brimmed straw hat graced his head. Being in his early seventies hadn't slowed him down at all and he put in a full day's work—and then some.

Today, a hog had been butchered for ham, loin, shoulder, ribs, bacon, and pork bellies. The hocks and feet had been saved for pickling and the rest of the animal now lay in pieces on a long table in front of Philip. He had sliced the various parts into smaller portions and one by one, dropped them into a large cast iron pot set over an open fire where water bubbled and boiled. In went heart, liver, kidneys, snout, ears, tail, entrails, even the whole head. In fact, everything from the pig except the oink was used in the making of pon haus, or scrapple, as it was sometimes called. Once the parts cooked properly, he removed the meat from the pot and any bones were discarded. Corn meal was added to form a kind of mush and the meat, now finely minced, returned to the pot along with thyme or sage or whatever herbs were available. Once the liquid was reduced and the mush congealed, it would be formed into a slab perhaps one half to one inch thick and sliced into squares to be pan fried in grease and served as a hearty breakfast or lunchtime meal. Nothing went to waste on the farm.

Looking deeper into the valley, past his fields and pastures, Philip could see the sparkling waters of a little creek that ran down it to join larger streams on their way to the Augwick. The low afternoon sun lit it with gold and it flashed and shimmered and seemed to leap off the dull greens and browns of the landscape like a smile. Coming up the road he saw his son, Isaac, leading a half dozen cows back from grazing to be milked. Curious, he thought, that Isaac has shown so much interest in the farm lately. He has a good business in town. Certainly he knows, thought Philip, that I am not yet so frail as to need the nurturing of his assistance. It's more work explaining everything to him than just doing it myself! But it is good to see him here on the farm. Very good.

Cows! Stupid animals, thought Isaac as he pulled open the barn doors. Not smart like pigs, All you had to do was figure out which cow was the leader cow and pull that one along with a piece of rope and all the others would line up behind it and follow. Getting them into the barn and into their stalls was all together another proposition, however. He pushed and tugged and the cows groaned and snorted until at last help arrived in the form of Peter Ranck, his wife, Anna, and their daughters, Ellie and Margaret, resident farm hands on his father, Philip's farm. Together they managed to array the cows in separate stalls and tie them for milking.

Was this the life for him, he wondered? In the darkness of the barn, with slivers of light slicing through cracks between slats and setting aglow airborne dust and bits of straw, he felt transported to another world—its mysteries hidden away in the blackness of corners where rotting wood sagged, in the unimaginable heights of the barn roof where strange aerial critters flitted in and out of holes punched there by unrelenting winds, and in the discordant mewing of the cows as skillful hands stroked and pulled the teats of their swollen udders. Mysterious, yet compelling: Isaac felt a connection to this world whose vitality was both real and unreal at the same time.

Cows in the barn, farm hands at work with the buckets, Isaac came out to where his father was stirring the mixture of pig offal and corn meal. The smell, just short of appetizing, mingled with the musty odor of trampled straw and manure wafting from the barn. Somehow, the combination was stimulating to Isaac—perhaps it was nostalgia for his younger days on the farm with his brothers and sister. Perhaps it was so indicative of that particular smell of the land which lived in one's soul and under one's fingernails that it shook away fatigue and woke up an innate awareness of belonging, of being part of nature, part of the land itself. At any rate, a glad feeling shown upon his face as he greeted his father.

"It's a good day, Father!"

"Isaac, you've been a great help to me these past few days."

"I'm more than happy to help, Father," Isaac answered.

"And it seems you have a million questions about farming. Things you didn't learn growing up here, I would guess."

"I just like to do things correctly. You've the experience. I'm just a beginner."

"A beginner, is it? Strange way of putting it. You are going into farming then?"

There was a long pause as Isaac examined his feet as if he were again a young boy who had been caught dawdling or shirking some important duty. His father looked away, attending to the scrapple mixture, then turned again toward Isaac saying, "There is more to this than just helping out, isn't there?"

"Father...I...I am considering..." But the words flowed unevenly, sticking upon guilt, uncertainty and frustration. Philip cocked his head. Perhaps, he thought, he would have to coax it out of his son with a few understanding words— understanding words he now fought hard to rationalize.

"Isaac, I know you respect your brothers."

"William and James. Of course I do. I named two of my sons after them. And one after you, Father."

"Of course. Well, William and James have worked the farm with me for years when you went your own way. And I thought, as William was the oldest, that he would take over the farm from me when I got older. But now he lives in Ohio.: Philip shook his head.

"Why on God's green earth he wanted to go there, I'll never know. Then James...well, James is not..."

"I know, Father. James has a condition that keeps him from being able to concentrate on anything for very long. He drifts in and out. He functions all right in ordinary activities, but he'd never be capable of running this farm. He needs car. You and Mother have provided that for so long."

"So you can appreciate that this sudden interest you have in farming is a joy to me. But..."

"But?"

"I could leave you the farm. You could start working it right now. Give your business to you sons. But I have to tell you that this farm is not what it used to be. The fields are too hilly to cultivate easily. The soil is old and tired—like me!"

"Oh, Father!"

"The price of seed is high and the yield is low. If you really want to farm, it might be better to look for other land. But not here. All the good land is gone. Go west. I hear many are going out there, where the land is cheap and the soil rich."

Isaac was stunned. "I don't know what to say. It's as if you've read my mind," he said. "But I don't want you to think I'm abandoning you. I want you and Mother to come with me wherever I end up."

"Isaac, Isaac. You know your mother and I are too rooted in our ways here. We're comfortable. We can't make a journey like that and keep our peace of mind. And there's the Church. I can't leave that."

"We'll start a new church out west."

"Give me a hand with this scrapple. There will be no more talk of this."

CHAPTER 5
THE LOVE FEAST

Shirleysburg, Pennsylvania, 26 May, 1845

Reverend Benjamin Bell, although he was fond of pontificating, restrained himself and commented only upon those aspects of the Love Feast that were significant, and might not be known to visitors to the church from other denominations, if any.

"Early Christians," he began, "gathered after the Pentecost to break bread together and celebrate the Lord's Supper. The sharing of food, prayer, conversation and song in our church is a continuation of this agape of the Apostles and may be thought of as the highest form of spiritual love. The food we offer here is not consecrated. This is not communion, but it is offered in the spirit of fellowship and devotion."

Mugs were passed throughout the congregation by some of the men, while sweet rolls in baskets were brought in by the women. As the food passed among those seated, hymns were sung by a choir and many joined their voices to the celebration.

John sipped from the mug, then turned to Will. "See, I told you it was tea," he said. The Grosh family took up an entire row of the wooden chairs in the church. Isaac and Catherine sat at the center, with the girls on their left and the boys on their right. By the time the mug had traveled across to Elizabeth, who was sitting at the end of the row, it was empty.

After a few hymns, the church goers engaged in quiet conversation among themselves. Officially, the topic was to be God's grace and the Christian life, but more often than not, the talk focused on farming or the price of hogs. In front of Isaac sat the Cornelius family. Amelia Cornelius was Catherine's older sister. She and her husband, Lewis, had six children, five of them boys. Dick, the oldest, was the same age as Philip and the girl, Becky, was a year younger than Will. The youngest child, Elias, was only three.

Isaac tapped Lewis on the shoulder. "Have you seen this?" he asked, handing him a creased flyer printed on yellowed newsprint. Lewis read:

Choice farm lands for sale! Now prepared to sell about 1,500,000 acres of choice farming lands in tracts of 40 acres and upwards, on long credits and at low rates of interest.

Isaac pointed out the bold print that said "**The Prices are from $6 to $30. Interest only 3 per-cent. TWENTY PR. CENT WILL BE DEDUCTED FROM THE CREDIT PRICE FOR CASH**."

"My nephew, Phillip, is already out there," Isaac told him. "He has bought farmland for one dollar fifty an acre. I'm planning to go next spring. You could come with us."

"Isaac, I am very interested in that idea. I don't know if I'd be ready by spring, but we'll see."

"I need to find a boat, or build one. My sons will help. People are traveling the rivers to the west. It is easier and quicker than by land."

"You'd need to get to the Allegheny and the Monongahela at Pittsburgh. The Ohio starts there. You could float all the way to Illinois, but then you'd have to travel up the Mississippi. Need a paddle wheeler for that."

"I'd look for a tow. I think I can build a flatboat easy enough. I can take the Juniata Canal from Huntingdon. There's a portage railway to Johnstown and the canal goes the rest of the way to Pittsburgh."

"I guess you could do it all right. If you can build a waterproof barrel, I guess you can build a waterproof boat!"

"Easy as Shoofly Pie!" said Isaac.

"Yeow!" yelled Becky Cornelius, Will having just pulled her pigtails. Heads turned and Isaac was forced to put on his most serious and threatening face.

"I'm sorry," Will said, caught between his father's and

his cousin's fierce stares.

"If I can find more families to go with me, I can build a bigger boat," Isaac said, returning to his conversation with Lewis Cornelius. "The Church promotes the spreading of the Brethren and the Word," he continued. "We can build a new community out there in the wilderness."

"Wilderness? Isn't it settled?"

"A bit. The land is virgin land for farming, though. And I hear there's a fellow out there invented a new plow that cleaves through the earth like a knife through butter."

"Well, I hope you're not hearing tall tales, that's all."

Isaac settled back in his chair as a new hymn was struck up by the choir.

> O Lord, Thy love's unbounded,
>   So sweet, so full, so free;
> My soul is all transported
>   Whene'er I think of Thee!
>
> Yet Lord, alas! what weakness
>   Within myself I find;
> No infant's changing pleasure
>   Is like my wandering mind.
>
> And yet Thy love's unchanging,
>   And doth recall my heart
> To joy in all its brightness,
>   The peace its beams impart.

After the service, the families exited the white washed church building and strolled along the road toward carriages and wagons parked in the shade of majestic maples and oaks. Horses snorted impatiently and the Grosh's mule, Sampson, bobbed his head in haughty indifference as they approached. Five year old Emma hung on the side of the wagon swinging her feet. "Let's play," she said to her older sister, Elizabeth. "I'll be the princess and you be... you be King Arthur."

"I can't be a king, Em, I'm a girl. I'll be Queen Jennifer."

"No," replied Emma, "I want to be the queen. You be the dragon."

"You're going to get splinters doing that. Better stop it."

"But I don't want to stop it. I'm the queen."

"You're a brat!"

"Girls!" said their mother. "Play nicely."

"When are we going home?" said Emma, whining.

"As soon as your Papa is done talking to Uncle Cornelius."

The enchantment of the sunny spring day seemed to mesmerize everyone as they left the church meeting. Groups of people clustered here and there along the avenue, continuing the conversations they'd begun during the Love Feast, perhaps more on the practical side of matters than on the religious. Bird song merged with the low chatter of humans and the rustling of the bridles of horses. Philip stood chatting with Dick Cornelius.

"So you're going to Illinois?" Dick asked.

"Looks that way. Think your Paw will come?"

"We've talked about it. My Ma is against it. I don't want to go either. I've got a girl here."

"Marry her and bring her along!"

"Oh, sure. Why don't you mind your own business."

"But, Dick, I think it would be great if your family came with us."

"Don't make trouble, Phil. We're not going. I wish your dad would stop trying to talk mine into going."

"Well, you're off your chump."

"Oh yeah?"

"Yeah!"

Then push came to shove and shove came to scuffle and scuffle led to rolling in the road. Clouds of dislodged dirt arose and were transformed by the wind into dust devils that whisked up the street like so many miniature tornadoes. Hands and feet protruded from the billowing nebula of grit as the tussling bodies twisted and turned. Elbows jabbed stomachs and fingers poked at eyes. Anyone observing the encounter, and that would include nearly the entire congregation of the United Brethren Church, would have thought they were witnessing a double murder. But the two tall men who stood passively over the battling cousins, and that would be Isaac Grosh and Lewis Cornelius, could hear the laughter emerging from the thickening cloud of dust, dirt and boys. When it all settled, and the two bedraggled ruffians stared meekly up at their frowning fathers, it was difficult to contain their mirth.

"This is not funny," scolded Isaac. "We'll discuss this later!"

"Off you go, before I throttle you," yelled Lewis Cornelius.

James sat on the side of the road grinning broadly. He chomped on huge chunk of sweet roll, stolen from the Love Feast left-overs. Up on the wagon, Catherine was arranging pillows to sit upon for the ride home. The girls were still dawdling next to the wagon, as impatient to be on their way as was Sampson, the mule.

Will had stood next to John under a tree, watching the entire episode. He said to no one in particular, "Well, it ought to be an interesting voyage!"

"Why do you say that?" asked James.

"I don't think Philip really wants to go."

"Oh? So that's why he's fighting with Dick?"

"You're too young to understand, Jimmy. Sometimes a person gets angry about something and shows it in a different way. Like fighting with somebody."

"Well, Pop said he could stay. Him and John too."

"They'd never do that. They know they should stay with the family until they're older. They have to help out."

"Well, I want to go. I want to fight Indians."

"You'll probably have to settle for just milking some cows or something. I don't think there are any Indians."

"Aw..." said James, finishing his sweet roll.

CHAPTER 6
ISAAC'S ARK

Huntingdon County, Pennsylvania, 15 March, 1846

The year 1845 had come and gone, leaving in its wake an angst about new beginnings that would only slowly subside for those who, like Catherine, had found acceptance of the inevitable, exacting and onerous. She conferred often with her sister, Amelia, who was determined that the Cornelius family would remain forever in Huntingdon County, in spite of her husband's desire to migrate. Catherine had been unable to dissuade Isaac in his determination. She grew to believe that Isaac's obsession with this odyssey to the west was unbreakable.

1845 had been fairly uneventful as years go. James K. Polk was the new President of the United States. Texas had been admitted to the union as the 28th state. Johnny Appleseed had died. It would be another cruel winter, breath freezing even when barely out of the mouth, eyelashes and beards hung with ice, hands numb, feet moments away from frost bite. Most of the fall of that year, Isaac watched boats.

The State of New York had opened its newly constructed Erie Canal in 1825, providing its huge manufacturing concerns with easy access to the Great Lakes. Commerce in Pennsylvania suffered until the Keystone State constructed its own canal and railway system connecting Philadelphia in the east to Pittsburgh in the west where the head waters of the Ohio river took barges loaded with goods as far as Chicago, Saint Louis and New Orleans. The Juniata branch of the canal ran parallel to the Juniata River, and so little Huntingdon had become a port, of sorts. The marina at Huntingdon often accommodated the canal barges for loading and unloading commodities and passengers. It was a great place to watch, and learn, about boats.

Isaac saw barges being pulled by horses along the canal paths. He saw keelboats, propelled by men with long poles, rafts piled with lumber, and flatboats of all sizes. It was the flatboat which interested him most. Boxy and difficult to navigate but inexpensive and easy to construct, it was designed to float down river with its cargo and then be sold, disassembled or abandoned, for otherwise, it would have to be towed for a return trip. It was superior to a simple raft as it had a hull and a draft only a foot or two in the water. It was covered either partially or completely for shelter from the elements, and the larger crafts carried livestock, barrel goods and whole families in relative comfort.

One day in late August of 1845, Isaac stood on the dock at the marina watching a crew of four flatboatmen unloading a mid-sized boat called a broadhorn. It appeared to be about fifty feet in length and less than twenty in width. It had an angled bow and stern and was maneuvered through the use of thirty foot long sweeps like paddles on each side and another long steering oar for a rudder at the stern. On the forward half of the deck was built a cabin and aft was a covered pen in which several pigs were noisily complaining. The open portion of the deck was filled with barrels and crates, and these were being hefted by the men who complained as loudly as their pigs.

"My last trip, this. I'm off."

"Ain't paying none too well neither. Been a month of Sundays since I could shake the elbow with a decent stake."

"Aw, ya dummkopf, yer a lazy ass."

"No, I'm saying. I've had it up to here. I'm winked out."

"We're all in that same boat. Hah! It's no joke!"

Isaac understood that the conflict unfolding before him would have no happy ending. Here were apparently three disgruntled men who'd not been paid and one overseer who was equally disenchanted with his lot. He saw an opportunity.

"Excuse me, my man," he said to the one who seemed to be in charge. "Can you tell me who owns this boat?"

"Well, I guess that would be me," answered the

flatboatman.

"Am I to understand you might be thinking of relinquishing yourself of this floating agony you call a vessel?"

"Well, I might at that. I might indeed be thinkin' like that."

"She looks sea worthy. What is she worth to you?"

"She cost me fifty dollars, sir. I'd be lookin' to get me forty back."

"I could offer you thirty and a good meal."

"That be hard cash? No script."

"That'd be cash. You get your cargo unloaded and I'll meet you at the Irishman's. You just leave it tied up here and come get your money."

One of the men turned to his boss. "Does that mean we'll be gettin' paid?"

"It does, and it means yer out of a job! Get movin' on those barrels, ya lazy bastard!"

Isaac had just committed a sizeable portion of his and Catherine's nest egg. He stopped by the bank on his way to the Irishman's pub to withdraw the thirty dollars. He asked for it in silver, as he knew the flatboatmen would not accept paper money or promissory notes. It was a risk, but here was a ready made boat, large enough for his family and belongings, and large enough to float the Allegheny, the Ohio, the Mississippi! It only remained for him to find adequate storage for the flatboat over the winter. Perhaps fix up its cabin with some amenities that Catherine and the girls would appreciate.

As he sat at a table at the pub he took the precaution of writing up a deed of ownership which he would have the flatboatman sign. He had met Philip and John in the street and had sent them to find a secure place to dry dock the boat until spring. He didn't want the flatboatmen to know where he had taken the boat once the money exchanged hands. It was not his custom to imbibe, but being elated at the prospect that his venture would succeed, he ordered a growler from the bartender to sip while he waited.

Philip and John had reasoned that if they took the flatboat back down the Juniata, they could branch off on Aughwick Creek and get the boat to within a few miles of their home in the German valley. They hadn't counted on the problem of getting a flatboat to travel upstream against the current, which would be the case once they reached Aughwich Creek.

"If the damn thing weren't so big, we could just carry it," said Philip.

"We could... if we disassembled it and took it by wagon, piece by piece," commented John.

"Doesn't that defeat the purpose of buying a boat that's already built?"

"Maybe. But if we rebuild it, we can be sure it's water tight and ship shape."

"Let's talk to Pop about it."

When they entered the pub, Isaac had just finished his transaction and was now the proud owner of a broadhorn flatboat. The flatboatman had swigged down a beer and exited the Irishman's establishment. The boys explained the situation and their solution to getting the boat home.

"That might not be such a crazy idea," said Isaac. "I'd hate to get half way to Illinois and have the blessed thing sink on us. We could have it in our back yard for the winter and not have to worry about anybody stealing it. Like that misanthrope I just gave a small fortune to! How long are those boards?"

"The way they build them, there are two gunwales that run the length and the bottom boards run the width. The sides can be pieced, so if that thing is fifty feet long, there's only a couple boards like that. The rest would stack on the wagon OK and I bet we could do it in only a couple of trips."

"Boy!" said Philip. "I never heard of un-building a boat!"

As soon as the snow melted the next spring, the Grosh's home became a shipyard. It turned out there were several rotted planks that needed replacing. The seams were planed and fitted by Will, and the old nails were discarded in favor of wooden pegs. They moved the finished boards to a flat landing along the Aughwick Creek and rebuilt the flatboat in two days time. It sat on logs which would act as rollers when the time came to launch the ark. The seams were caulked with tar, although Will maintained they were so tightly reengineered they'd not leak. The cabin was fitted with a fold-down table and a cook stove. The covered animal pen was repurposed as a latrine and fitted with solid walls. There was a tub for bathing, although the water to fill it would be drawn from the river. The remaining deck would be adequate for the family's belongings packed in barrels, and the roofs of the cabin and latrine would provide a day deck which, for them, was as fancy as any ocean liner's.

The day Philip, John and Will were beginning to lay out the gunwales, Isaac was in town. Dick Cornelius appeared, agitated and nervous. Asked if he had come to help with the construction, Dick was momentarily silent. At last he explained that, because his mother was now pregnant again, the Cornelius family would not be voyaging with the Groshes. But his father had told him to go west by himself, to scout out the territory and find a suitable farm they might acquire. This he opposed, being in love with Sara Ann Bollinger and unwilling to part from her. But his father's command was final and nonnegotiable.

"But also I have to warn you," said Dick, "the sheriff has been up and down the river looking for a stolen flatboat."

"What's that to do with us?" asked Philip.

"It seems some men sold a flatboat to a local last fall and it didn't belong to them."

"Does he know about our boat?"

"He knows you are building a boat. So I don't think he suspects it could be the same one. But I'd be cautious."

"Please, Dick, don't ever let our father know about this! He's so honest he'd probably give the boat back and be ruined in the process."

Open barrels filled the house at German Valley. Catherine packed the china dishes and cups in wood shavings. Mary Jane and Elizabeth folded clothing and filled another barrel. Emma and Katy saw to the dolls and picture books, fighting for space with James who insisted on bringing his collection of toy soldiers. Other barrels were needed for foodstuffs: flour, pilot bread, coffee, rice, sugar, dried beans, corn meal...anything that would keep. The baking soda, vinegar, salt, kitchen utensils, bible, and, of course, a flask of whiskey for medicinal purposes, were placed in a smaller crate that could be accessed easily. Just before leaving they would fill another barrel with clear clean water from their well—possibly the last fresh water they would see for a month. Tools, ropes, canvas, fire wood and other everyday items would be stacked on the open deck. The only luxury item Isaac was bringing was his prized rocking chair.

Philip and Dick stood in the rushing creek water up to their knees and pulled and tugged on ropes attached to the bow of the flatboat. As they pulled, Will and John pushed and the flatboat rolled off the bank and into Aughwick Creek with a glorious splash. Cheers went up from the boys and Isaac looked on, stoic as always, but secretly elated. They tethered the boat to a tree and laid a wide plank between the shore and the boat. James was walking Sampson down to the bank with the wagon full of barrels and crates. These they began loading onto the flatboat. With each barrel or crate or chest, the boat sank lower into the creek until suddenly, it sat on the bottom.

"What in the Sam Hill?" cried James.

"Do not swear, James," scolded Isaac.

"But look! The boat's on the bottom!"

"Is it on a sand bar?" asked John.

"Not likely. We've had no rain for a week and the water's low. Looks like the boat takes more water than we got!" answered Philip.

"What do we do now?"

"Well, I don't know, but it seems to me, we'll have to unload this stuff."

"Aw, doggone it!"

"What'd I tell you, James?"

"Well, anyway," said John, "at least we got it in the water."

CHAPTER 7
INTREPID MARINERS

The Juniata River and Canal, 15 - 16 March, 1846

"Well," said Will, "it's a really good thing we didn't sell Sampson as yet."

The unloading of the flatboat went more slowly than the loading had, the esprit de corps having been dampened somewhat by the stranding of their vessel. Once unloaded, the flatboat floated freely and down the creek they went, followed by Sampson, pulling the fully loaded wagon along the shore and, ironically, making better time. It was late afternoon when they reached the Juniata. Here they tied the boat and again swung the plank across for reloading their cargo.

"We'll wait for morning before embarking," Isaac said. "The women can spend one last night in the house."

"Dick and I will spend the night on the boat," offered Philip.

"We'll bring the rest of our belongings and the food tomorrow."

"I have a question," said John. "Did you notice that the river here flows south-east? The canal is north-west, up at Huntingdon. Will we be able to paddle this thing upstream?"

"Not at all. What we will do is get a tow from one of the river boats that pass by here. We may have to wait a bit." Isaac answered.

The plaintive cry of a mourning dove woke them the next day. Catherine cooked a hearty breakfast of griddlecakes and they ate these with the last of their fresh bacon. Amelia Cornelius was at the door and a tearful goodbye was said between the sisters. Her second oldest son, John, was with her.

"Johnny can bring your wagon back for you," said Amelia. "I'm going to miss you."

"And I you. When is the blessed event to be?" asked Catherine.

"I figure around October. You see, we just couldn't be on that boat with you. It's enough to be sending Dick along. I'm not pleased with that either."

Catherine sympathized with Amelia, but there was something she hadn't told her, or even Isaac, for that matter. She too was pregnant and expecting at nearly the same time. If Isaac knew about the baby now, he would cancel the trip, she was sure. It might have been to her benefit to tell him, but she would feel guilty to derail Isaac's grand plan. Besides, she had survived giving birth to nine children. So far. And she felt fine, even energized, now that the trip was underway.

And so the last of their belongings was gathered up and they piled into the wagon. Catherine took a last look at the house where she and Isaac had made a home for so long. Now it would be occupied by tenants working for Isaac's father. Tears welled up in her eyes as the wagon rolled down the lane and headed toward the flatboat moored on the Juniata. On her lap, wrapped in paper, were the last of the griddlecakes, cold now, but they undoubtedly would be relished by Philip and Dick.

Two riverboats had steamed past them before a third acknowledged their "Halloo!" Would they tow them up to Huntingdon? Could they pay for the tow? It was the first among many lessons in river navigation, and an expensive one, for a silver dollar passed across to the steamboat's captain before a line was thrown and the flatboat pulled swiftly up river.

A pair of blue herons took flight from the low bushes on the opposite shore, their "cawk, cawk, cawk" barely audible over the chugging of the steamboat. The smooth silken surface of the Juniata was churned and rippled by the wake of the steamboat, its paddle splashing and throwing a heavy green mist into the air that fell back onto the flatboat. John had never seen the river from this perspective: the rust colored bluffs of shale and sandstone, the drifting trunks and branches of trees torn down by wind or lightning looking like dead soldiers floating in the River Styx. Wood ducks ushered their ducklings into the shelter of the shoals as the boats steamed by.

Emma was bored. She had tucked her jump rope into the pocket of her smock and she now withdrew this and climbed the ladder to the upper deck. She tied her skirts up and began skipping rope chanting:

> Miss Mary Mack Mack Mack
> All dressed in black black black
> With silver buttons buttons buttons
> Up and down her back back back.
> She asked her mother mother mother
> For six pence pence pence
> To see the elephant elephant elephant
> Jump the fence fence fence
> He jumped so high high high
> He touched the sky sky sky
> And he never came back back back
> Till the fourth of July ly ly

Hearing the thud thud thud of the girls feet and the snap snap snap of the skip rope on the roof above, Catherine rushed out the door of the cabin, appalled to see Emma skipping rope on the upper deck.

"Emma Hattie Grosh!" she called. "Get down here this instant! Stop that foolishness. You could fall into the river and be drowned!"

"Oh, Mama, I'm careful. There's just not enough room down there."

"There's no railings up there. I don't want you or Katy to go up there, you understand me?"

"Yes, Mama," said Emma, descending the ladder. By this time, a varied assortment of passengers had assembled on the deck of the steamboat and were entertaining themselves by watching the little drama on the flatboat. A man in a derby hat and bright red vest waved. Emma saw this as her foot found the first rung of the ladder and she waved back.

"Emma!" scolded Catherine.

As they drew closer to Huntingdon, makeshift piers appeared along the shore, a row boat or a canoe tied to the pilings. They could see dwellings that were mere shacks with pens for pigs or sheep. Trees thinned out and farms were visible, rolling back from the river on gently sloping land. Then, gradually, larger structures were evident: a grist mill, a warehouse, a foundry. Now they saw the canal running along side the river, saw it cross Standing Stone Creek on a high wooden aqueduct. They were nearing the next leg of their journey.

North of the town of Huntingdon, the Pennsylvania Canal route hopped back and forth between the canal and the Little Juniata using a series of dams and locks. They approached an entrance lock, having cast off from the riverboat, paddling the flatboat by dipping the sweeps into the river and pulling with all their might against the current. Here they encountered the lock tender, a burly man in soiled trousers and billowing shirttails who halted their progress by waving a red flag at them and hollering, "You there, tie off at the pier."

The canal was different from the river in many ways. It was narrower, more crowed, slower with obstacles like locks and aqueducts, and, most significantly, it was not free. The toll, the lock tender informed Isaac, was twenty-five cents per mile for a boat carrying passengers, or, if you wanted to figure it differently, ten cents per mile for the boat and one cent per mile for each passenger over eight years of age. Isaac quickly figured in his head that they had eleven people aboard, of whom two, Emma and Katy, were under eight years old, and so settled on nineteen cents per mile with the lock tender. He was given a paper which stated his entry point to the canal and told he would have to pay when he got to the Allegheny Portage Railway. The trip was getting to be expensive.

They were towed by mule through slack water where the river was dammed, then along the canal from lock to lock. A young boy led the mule, his feet bare and his neck and shoulders sunburned. There was nothing for the intrepid mariners to do but to sit and watch the embankment roll by at a snail's pace. The canal authorities had imposed a speed limit on boats of four miles per hour. Some of the bigger commercial boats exceeded this when they could, but were ultimately slowed again waiting for their turn at the lock.

Outside of Alexandria they entered a lock. It was nearly twice the length of their flatboat but left them only a few feet on either side where stone walls rose six feet above their heads. A wooden gate closed behind them and water was diverted into the lock from a holding pool. As the boat rose upward they could see the lock tender's cabin a few yards away. A woman was bending over in a garden where hollyhocks swayed in the gentle wind. A small dog barked at them. When they had risen to the level of the other side of the lock, the front gate opened, the mule surged forward, the slack rope tightened and they moved once again along the canal.

Philip, Dick and John were sitting on barrels on the lower deck. John broached the subject with Dick as to his girl, Sara Ann Bollinger. Was he going to marry her, he wanted to know.

"I'll ask her father when I return. She'll have me, I know it."

"Have you ever kissed her?"

"I have. I seen her in her bloomers, too."

"You haven't!"

"I have. She's a stunner, I tell you. And she thinks I'm gallant."

"Have you... you know... touched her?"

"Say, mind your own business!"

"Just askin."

They passed the canal town of Alexandria and continued through the hills and valleys, changing elevation through the locks. The canal followed the river as it broke through mountain passes and collected tributaries. Great stands of timber loomed against slopes of granite, then gave way to fertile fields where settlers had burned the forests in order to clear the land for farming. The natural history which was written on that terrain was now being amended by the careless pen of man.

Evening was upon them by the time they reached Williamsburg. They were midway between Huntingdon and Holidaysburg, where the canal would meet the Allegheny Portage Railway. They tied up for the night, just off the diamond of the town. Williamsburg sat in an oxbow made by the river, nurtured by a natural spring that turned the wheels of its grist mills. The log cabins of ordinary folk stood along side the homes of the more affluent which were constructed of hand-made brick. Stores, liveries, warehouses, eateries and taverns lined the street along the canal, testifying to the town's dependence on the waterway.

"May we go explore the town?" John asked his father. "We've been cooped up in this boat all day long."

"You all can go, but stay together. Mother and I will stay here with Katy. Be back in one hour. We'll have dinner then."

The children scrabbled over the side and ran off down the street, eager to peer through store windows. Isaac unlashed his rocker from the railing of the flatboat and took Katy in his lap. Catherine returned to the cabin where she began pounding a cone of sugar in a mortar. She sifted this and added it to the corn meal mush she had boiling in a cast iron pot on the cook stove. There was some bread left and coffee she would heat up. A meager meal, but hearty.

The children returned to the flatboat, winded and happy at having stretched their legs. Isaac counted heads. "Where are James and Mary Jane?" he said.

CHAPTER 8
SHIP OF THE ALLEGHENIES

Allegheny Portage Railway, 17 May, 1846

The flatboat waited in line in the canal basin at Hollidaysburg for its turn to be transferred to the Allegheny Portage Railway. Isaac carefully watched as a canal boat, constructed of two long sections which could be detached to fit on the train, were floated onto flat cars submerged in the basin. Once secured, the cars were pulled out of the water by a stationary steam locomotive. Another engine pulled the cars rapidly a short distance to a shed at the foot of the first incline. Here there was a continuous cable running over rollers between the tracks. This was powered by another stationary steam locomotive under a shed at the top of the incline. The cars would be hooked to this cable and pulled up a steep slope nearly four miles long in less than an hour. There were five inclines going up the eastern side of the mountain and five descending the western slopes.

As Isaac watched this his mind wandered, reliving the events of the previous evening in Williamsburg when James and Mary Jane had not shown up for dinner. His son, John, had offered to search for them. "I have a hunch," he had said. After he had been gone several minutes, Isaac decided to send Philip and Dick along after him. You could never tell what might happen in a rough and rugged canal town like Williamsburg.

When the group of Grosh children and Dick Cornelius had stood gaping through the window of Stoke's Mercantile Emporium on High Street, James had grasped Mary Jane by the arm and whispered, "Come with me."

"Where are we going?" she asked.

"You'll see," James said. And pulled her around the

corner and down an alley toward a darkened street where only a single building showed lights. A wooden sign hung over the door announcing that this establishment was "Limey's Ale House and Eatery, Fine Spirits and Gastronomical Delights."

"We can't go in there," objected Mary Jane. She was just 12 and he 14, but James was oblivious to this circumstance.

James eased open the door and pulled Mary Jane through into a smoky, crepuscular, cavernous space where men were seated at long tables raising steins and voices in a celebratory commotion. The children slipped unseen into a booth and surveyed the scene which both had only imagined from school yard tales. There was a man seated at a piano, pounding out what appeared to be a familiar melody and singing:

>A man whose name is Johnny Sands,
>Had married Betty Hague,
>And though she brought him gold and lands,
>She prov'd a terrible plague,
>For Oh! she was a scolding wife,
>Full of caprice and whim.
>He said, that he was tired of life,
>And she was tired of him.
>And she was tired of him,
>And she was tired of him.
>
>Says he "Then I will drown myself—
>The river runs below,"
>Says she, "Pray do you silly elf
>I wished it long ago,"
>Says he, "Upon the brink I'll stand,
>Do you run down the hill,
>And push me in with all your might,"
>Says she my love I will,"
>Says she "my love I will,"
>Says she "my love I will."

Mary Jane was shocked and delighted all at once. James beamed saying, "See, I told you it was something!"

They sat, unobserved by the denizens of the tavern and watched a bar maid carrying a tray of mugs through the crowded room. As she passed a nearby table, a man thrust out his leg and tripped the girl sending mugs of beer flying and the girl sprawling onto the dirty floor. His cronies laughed and slapped the table in glee. James frowned.

"Oh that poor girl," said Mary Jane.

"The bastard!" shouted James.

"What did you say?" said the man who had tripped the bar maid, approaching the booth where James and Mary Jane sat.

"I said, you bastard!" James replied, at which the man grabbed James by his shirt front and jerked him into an upright position, not quite standing, but definitely teetering. From across the room the booming voice of the bartender yelled:

"Hey, get those kids out of here! And you," he said to the girl, who was now picking herself up from the floor, "clean up that mess!"

Philip and Dick searched the empty streets, unsure of which direction John had taken. At last they came to the alley beside the tavern and witnessed a sight that displeased them. Three beefy ruffians surrounded James and John. One of the men was holding Mary Jane at bay, his arm straightened, as she swung wildly at him and let loose with a series of epithets which were hardly complimentary. In fact, Philip was amazed that his sister knew such words, much less that she could utter them with such eloquence.

"Looks like it'll be more of an even fight, now," Philip said.

It was, of course, James that started the debacle. The arrival of Philip and Dick might have persuaded the men to return to the tavern, but James, heartened by the reinforcements, charged at the nearest antagonist, throwing him off balance. The man fending off Mary Jane gave her a shove and turned on James, throwing him to the ground. The third man ran at John, grabbing him in a bear hug that took the wind out of him. The three men hadn't yet seen Philip and Dick who rushed at them, fists swinging.

John wriggled out of his attacker's grasp and landed a haymaker on his jaw. A sucker punch, they called it, and the man collapsed in a heap. Philip and Dick pummeled the other men with a ferociousness that would cause them, much later, to remark, "Them farm boys sure packs a wallop!" The fray lasted only a short time as the men from the tavern, already three sheets to the wind, surmised that resuming the quenching of their thirsts was more productive than fisticuffs with these battling maniacs. Especially the girl. After their retreat, blood was wiped from noses, dirt shaken from shirt tails and the group hurried back to the flatboat, hoping their dishevelment would pass unnoticed.

It didn't. Isaac's wrath flared like burning gases erupting from a volcano, his voice as thunderous as God's rebuking Moses from the burning bush. But his anger soon faded as Catherine's touch on his shoulder and the tears in the eyes of Mary Jane and James stilled him and shifted his perspective to relief that they were unharmed.

"This should be a lesson for you all," he said. "Now let's have a good meal and look forward to tomorrow."

As the flatboat, now fastened to a railroad car, began its climb up the first incline, the barrels and crates on the lower deck started to slide. There was a sudden yelp and a strange figure jumped into view. Standing before them in a tattered coat and thread bare trousers was a young black man, his hands held high in a gesture of surrender. Isaac stared in disbelief.

"You there, what are you doing on our boat?" he said. The man looked confused, seemed to consider, then replied:

"I's got no money fo' de fare, Suh. I hopes yo don' mind me taggin' along wit ya."

Philip nudged his father. He whispered, "Father, he's a runaway slave. We could get in a lot of trouble with him on board."

"Philip," said Isaac, "you know as I do that slavery is an abomination to the Lord's Word."

"Yes, but..."

"I's not a slave, Suh," said the man. I's jus' poor an' travelin' alone like. I can hep yo wit drivin' the boat, I can."

"There's no drivin' to be done right now, fellow. We're on a train. I guess you're to be with us, at least to Johnstown. Can't very well set you off in the mountains."

"Thank you, Suh. I sure 'preciates it."

Philip gave his father a discouraging look. John and Will had just come from inside the cabin and were startled to see the black man on the deck. After their experiences the night before they were apprehensive and naturally suspicious of strangers, especially ones materializing on the deck of a boat that was "sailing" up a mountain. One by one, the rest of the family and Dick appeared and each in turn registered surprise and not a little anxiety at the newcomer's presence.

The journey up the mountain was a series of steep inclines separated by short distances of flat terrain where they were pulled by a small locomotive. The mountain air was sweet and crisp. Towering hemlocks lined the hills where streams flowed cold over glistening rocks and cascaded over small waterfalls. They saw a deer posed still as a statue, her head turned toward the impossible sight of a boat traveling up the mountain side. Where the tracks skirted close to a sheer precipice they could imagine the cable breaking and the train plunging into the depths of the chasm below.

During the trip to the summit, James sat along side Jacob Green, for that was the black man's name, and listened to his story. He insisted he was a free man, but James doubted this, due to details that emerged from the tale. Jacob Green had come from a plantation in Virginia and made his way to Holidaysburg traveling on what was called "the Underground Railroad." He and two other slaves had been pursued by the son of the plantation owner. In Holidaysburg they were recaptured, but as Jacob was being led away by horseback, a crowd of people, believing him a kidnap victim, urged him to jump from the horse and escape. He ran into a barbershop owned by a freed black man who ushered him out the back door. Somehow he made it to the canal basin and hid in the Groshes' flatboat.

James thought this was wonderfully romantic, overlooking the obvious pitfalls of a fugitive life. Although Pennsylvania was a free state, escaped slaves could be pursued under the laws of other states like Virginia and returned to their owners. Slave hunters were rarely helped in their pursuit of runaways by Pennsylvanians, however. Once across the border, runaways like Jacob Green considered themselves free men but were always in danger of recapture.

They reached the summit of the mountain. The air was cold and laced with the fresh smell of pine forests. Jacob Green stood looking out at the immensity of the Allegheny, with its deep valleys and tree-draped hills. A tear found its way to his eye. "What's the matter, Jake?" inquired James.

"I's been to the mountain," said Jacob Green. "I's free at last."

The descent was as rapid as climbing the mountain had been. The boat seemed to dangle precariously as it traversed the inclines. Near the bottom there was a long, dark tunnel, through which the younger children screamed and yelled to hear echoes, but these were drowned out by the clatter and rumble of the train. In all, they had spent only about six hours crossing the mountain, a technological feat unequaled anywhere in the world. As they approached the Johnstown canal basin, Isaac saw several men, one toting a shotgun, waiting at the dock.

"Jake! Quickly! Hide," he shouted. Jacob Green crawled on hands and knees and reached the shelter of the latrine just as the man with the shotgun leaped onto the flatboat.

"There's a darkey on this barge," he said. "I mean to arrest him."

CHAPTER 9
THE SLAVE'S TALE

Johnstown, Pennsylvania, 17 May, 1846

Johnstown, a thriving river port and iron producing city, sat in the apex of the confluence of the Little Conemaugh and Stone Creek rivers. It connected the Allegheny Portage Railway with the Western Branch of the Pennsylvania canal system and was the gateway to Pittsburgh and beyond. In 1889 the South Fork Dam on the Little Conemaugh River would collapse during a torrential rain and more than two thousand people would die in one of the worst flood disasters in Pennsylvania history. But today, there was not a cloud in the sky and the placid waters of the canal basin lapped lazily against the flatboat, rocking it gently.

A man in a long coat and slouch hat stood on the deck of the flatboat, his arm cradling a nasty looking shotgun. The pencil thin mustache on his upper lip gave a sinister twist to the smirk with which he surveyed the boat and its inhabitants. He exuded an air of authority in his stance that seemed solid although the flatboat rocked in the water. It was clear that the man meant business, and the business, for the Groshes, would be less than rewarding if he had his way.

"What are you doing on my boat," Isaac questioned. "You have no right here."

"I have every right, Suh! I am Colonel Parsons of Hampshire County, Virginia. I am seeking my runaway slave."

"This is Pennsylvania, Sir! There are no slaves here."

"This is my law," said Parsons, patting the shotgun. "I mean to search your boat." The determination of the man was frightening. His belief that he would be obeyed was so strong it almost convinced Isaac and his sons to allow the Colonel to proceed. Almost.

Isaac nodded to Philip and Dick Cornelius who were standing across the deck from him. They moved swiftly toward the Colonel and each seized him by an arm and a leg. "You, Sir, are no Southern gentleman!" said Philip as they hoisted him up and over the railing, dropping him with a great splash into the canal. Parsons sputtered and cursed as he swam to the shore.

"Keep your powder dry," shouted Isaac, tossing the shotgun after him.

When they were under way again, Isaac shouted to Jacob Green that it was safe to vacate the latrine. "I's so scared I hafta use the pot, Suh," came the reply. There were over 100 miles of canal between them and Pittsburgh and 68 more locks, a tunnel over 800 feet long and many aqueducts. Isaac was nervous that they might encounter the Colonel again waiting for them at one of the locks. When Jacob finally emerged from his hiding place, Isaac said:

"You best come with us all the way to Pittsburgh. But take caution as we approach the locks."

"I will, Suh." replied Jacob.

"In fact, if you wish to stay with us all the way to Illinois, I could probably use you on the farm I'm going to purchase."

"Thank you, but I believe I gets off at Pittsburgh. I has friends there what will hep me. I do 'preciate it though, Suh."

The canal followed the Conemaugh River as it snaked its way to the town of Freeport on the Allegheny River just north of Pittsburgh. Encountering its many oxbows, the engineers of the canal had opted to bridge the loops of the river with wooden aqueducts. As they crossed upon one of these, little Katy sat on Jacob Green's lap and Emma and Elizabeth huddled around him as he sang them spirituals and field songs. He sang:

> Go down Moses
> Way down in Egypt land
> Tell ole Pharaoh

To let my people go

When Israel was in Egypt land
Let my people go
Oppressed so hard dey could not stand
Let my people go

"Thus spoke de Lord," bold Moses said
"If not, I'll smite your first born dead
Let my people go

"Dis song," Jacob told them, "is 'bout my people. It tell us to go from the plantation. To ran 'way. I's done it, now I's free. I'm gwine to Canada someday."

"Canada? What's Canada," asked Emma.

"Canada is de promised land. Dey be no slaves der."

"Papa says our people were prosecuted too," said Emma.

"Persecuted," corrected Elizabeth. "We fled from France in... in... a long time ago. We were being killed because of our religion."

"We's had our religion too," said Jacob. We's gwine to Jesus 'cause dey make us. But we still have de Spirit."

"What's the Spirit?"

"It when we dance and feel it move through us. Massa don' like that, no way. Now Jesus is Spirit."

"Sing us another!" And Jacob started to sing:

De talles' tree in Paradise,
De Christian call de tree of life;
And I hope dat trump might blow me home
To de new Jerusalem.
Blow your trumpet, Gabriel,
Blow louder, louder;
And I hope dat trump might blow me home
To de new Jerusalem.

Katy clapped her hands in time to the song. Will, James and Mary Jane had joined the little group listening to Jacob. James asked. "Did they beat you?" Will gave him a kick.

"Beat me? Oh deys a beat us fo' sure. I could tell you

stories, only I's afeared of scarin' the lil' one."

"She'll be all right. Go on."

"Well, I recollect a furst time I seen a floggin' was my gram mama what had been caught at a prayer meetin'."

"You couldn't go to church?"

"It was as I say, the Spirit movin' us to dance. Dey 'fraid we up and rebel at 'em if we gwine to meetin' at night. The overseer, he tie her hands wit rope to a tree and bare her back. Forty lashes he give her an' we hadda watch this, jus' lil' chilun."

"But an old lady?"

"Dint give 'em no mind if ole or young. Sometimes it be jus' a misunderstandin' like. One gal, see, give an answer Massa don' get right and she beat fer it. It's worse, though, is sellin'. You see your daddy or your brudder sold away and never see 'em 'gain.

"Mostly we live together all in a cabin, brothers, sisters, uncles, aunts. But we families get broke up when Massa needs de money. Dey don' never work at anythin' but cruelty. Can't work in the field wit the black man, no Suh. Dat white man be looked down upon if he do. Dey talkin' dat de Bible it say only the black man is fit to work. I sez dey lazy and mean and feared of us.

"An' we smarter than dey is. Why, I recollect one time when some pigs was missing and the overseer he went to search all our cabins. Dey be 200 lashes for a stealin' a pig from Massa, you see. So this gal, she had the pig all cut up and hear him comin' to search. So she throw de pig, blood, guts and all into dis vat of persimum—dats beer, you know. An' de overseer he search but don't find no pig. So he sees dis persimum and say to her, 'Yo' give me some beer, gal.' An' she draw him a bowl full. He drink and ax for another, sayin' 'This the best beer I ever had!'"

The youngsters laughed at the story. "I was wupped once at school," said James.

"Ha! They used to break in the switches on you!" said Will.

"De furst time I try to escape, I got 100 lashes," continued Jacob. "Dey take the pepper and make a paste which dey rubs into where de lash cuts yer back. You has to pull on a shirt soaked in oil to go to work in de mornin'.

53

De second time I don' get caught."

"How'd you escape this time?" asked Will.

"It like dis. See de furst time I jus' run. An' dey got de dogs after me. I'd a had to climb a tree an' thas how dey got me. Dem dogs was so vicious, dey had to whip 'em jus' to keep 'em from tearing us limb from limb. So I was punished and treated pretty badly for a time to come. One day a man, a planter over next county come. He's a abolitionary, but Massa, he don' know this. Anyway I's talkin' to him and told him I wanna go to Canada so bad. Well, he says to me that if I don' tell no one, not even my Mama, he will hep me. I get in his wagon under some ole rugs and he takes me to another place. 'Go with this man,' he say. And I shook dis planter's hand and thank him.

"At the other man's house I stay for a time and am fed and hid. Then I's taken by a little skiff boat up the riber to a place and another man take over my well being. Dis is de 'Underground Railroad', they tells me, but I ain't see no engine or tracks. Well, I finally gets across to Pennsylvania but I hears dat Massa an' his son is on my trail. I borrowed a horse, and dats when de son apprehend me. Got loose an' ran again. I hid in yo' boat, as you know, an' here I is."

That night, Dick Cornelius and Philip slept out on the deck along side Jacob Green. They were concerned that the Colonel might still be in pursuit of Jacob. In the morning, it was the plan to exchange the mule for a fresh animal, and the boy that led the mule to return with a boat going in the opposite direction. They learned that a new boy hadn't arrived at the lock tender's house, and that a delay was likely. Philip volunteered to lead the new mule and planned to exceed the speed limit during this leg of the journey.

The mule's name, Philip had been told, was Noah. As he led Noah along the narrow path, Philip thought of their old mule, Sampson, of the trips along the Aughwick to deliver barrels to Huntingdon. He thought of the blue rocks that seemed ready to tumble down upon them from the ridges where bald eagles nested and falcons cruised the updrafts. Of the singing of the woodcocks in the stands of aspen and dogwood. Of the clear, rippling brooks that fed the Aughwick through which Sampson splashed. And the sound of wagon wheels in dire need of greasing.

He wondered, would he miss all that? He might have stayed, taken over the cooperage, found a girl the way Dick Cornelius had, settle down. Here he was, leading a strange mule along a gravel path toward...was that a tunnel? A peninsula of tall ridge land within the oxbow of the river called Bow Ridge had been hollowed out to form a long tunnel through which, to Philip's amazement, the canal was routed. First, there was a stone aqueduct that spanned the river with magnificent arches. Then 800 feet of darkness with a skittish mule whose footfalls clanked and echoed off the moss covered tunnel walls. Time to think.

At Saltsburg they obtained a new boy to lead the mule. There were a few stretches of travel in the river, now called the Kiskiminetas, where dams created slack water, but many more locks stood between them and the Allegheny River. Since Johnstown, they had dropped nearly 500 feet in elevation. Philip saw his father standing at the rail. Isaac traced the flight of a red-tailed hawk in the sky above. Philip touched his shoulder.

"Father, can we talk?"

"Of course, Philip."

"I've been thinking. Wondering if I made a mistake in coming."

"You have regrets?"

"Yes, I'm considering maybe returning. I can get a canal boat at Pittsburgh."

"Are you homesick already? You know the cooperage is sold."

"I might get a job there. Or something else."

"It has always been your decision, Philip. I would be sad if you left us, especially now, but you have your own life to live."

"Thank you, Father. I will think some more about it."

Near Freeport, the Kiskiminetas flowed into the Allegheny. Here, the canal crossed to the western bank and continued south toward Pittsburgh. An aqueduct of well over a thousand feet carried boats back across the Allegheny and into the city proper. River and canal traffic was thick with steam driven packet boats and barges, even flatboats with sails hoisted to pull them faster along the river current. Isaac's flatboat now sat rocking in a small canal basin, their journey through the Pennsylvania Main Line Canal, complete.

"If I never see another lock again," said Isaac, "it will be too soon!"

CHAPTER 10
THE CITY OF BRIDGES

Pittsburgh, Pennsylvania, 19 May, 1846

Gasper Petersen, of Petersen's General Store, eyed the black man suspiciously. As he waited on the woman accompanied by the negro, he reflected that there were rewards for capturing runaway slaves. Perhaps he'd mention this one to a man he knew. Maybe he'd make a little extra cash today.

Catherine had ventured out along the wharves and the trash filled streets of Pittsburgh to buy supplies. She was nearly out of salt, that all important element of life, and needed sugar, flour and corn meal. She was now giving in to the impulse to acquire fresh eggs and bacon, an extravagance, but sorely desired. Jacob Green had come with her and her two children, James and Mary Jane, saying to her, "I's wanna do sumpin' fo' yo' afore I leaves, yo' been so kind to me. I can tote the vittles."

Gasper Petersen's focus remained on Jacob Green so he didn't notice the boy wandering down the aisle where tools and other dry goods were displayed. James explored the store, the largest he had even been in, with the delight only young boys can generate in otherwise mundane circumstances like shopping. He looked at saws and axes, equestrian tack and horse blankets. He wandered down the aisle tracing his finger through the dust on glass topped counters. Then his glaze fell upon it—the golden fleece in all its shining glory. There, under the glass counter, lay a Colt Paterson Five Shot Revolver.

It wasn't the dust covered relic that old Ben Pergrin had once let him hold. No, this was pristine, oiled and ready for action. James quickly looked around. No one would see him if he just slipped behind the counter and..."James! Come along. We're going now," came his mother's summons. With the stealth and agility of a squirrel scampering around the back of a tree, James grabbed the hand gun, took an extra microsecond to scope up a box of shells, and stuffed his ill-gotten goods under his shirt.

Back at the flatboat, Jacob Green prepared to embark on the next leg of his quest for Canada. The girls hugged him, saying, "We love you, Jake!" The black man smiled. He shook Isaac's hand with a vehemence that could have pumped water. The boys surrounded him. "Don't go," each said in his own way: James with an elfish grin, Will with a serious and gracious manner, John with incredulity and concern, Philip with sympathy and understanding, and Dick Cornelius with guarded anxiety.

"I wish you'd come with us to Illinois, Jake," said Isaac. "There's no slavery there, just like Canada. Only self-imposed slavery to hard work on the land, and I know you aren't afraid of that."

"My mind's made up, Mr. Isaac. I started on this railroad thing and I intend gwine to Canada. There's a sweet gal there waitin' on me. I caint disappoint her."

Jacob Green slipped over the side of the flatboat and began walking along the road toward the part of town known as "the point" where the rivers converged. As his slim form disappeared around the corner of a building Philip turned to his father. "I'm leaving now too, Father," he said.

"I know. But Philip, before you go, your mother...she's in the cabin. You need to talk to her about this."

Philip entered the interior of the cabin where Catherine was folding and putting away the blankets and sleeping clothes from the night before. The darkness in the small living space was pierced by golden light that beamed through the openings that served as windows and set motes of swirling dust aglow. There seemed a heaviness there, as if the walls and ceiling contracted: a quiet, empty, diminishing void that weighted down the soul. Philip was at a loss to comprehend the sense of despair that came upon him as he prepared to beseech acceptance from this woman who had raised and nurtured him, whom he was about to abandon.

"Mother, I..."

"I know, Philip. You must go. You have a life to live."

"You understand?"

"No, Philip, I don't understand, not really. We are a family, we're strong and true and live by our wits and the grace of God, but together...always together. You may leave us, but you'll be a part of us. I...I feel...I'm about to lose another child! Of course, I don't understand."

"Oh, Mother, you'll not lose me. I'll become rich and I'll come to see you in Illinois. You'll see."

"Come over here, Philip. I want to give you something." From a small chest Catherine brought out a long heavy object. It caught a beam of light and sparkled brightly. "This is a solid silver serving spoon that Grandma Burns gave us on our wedding day. It will pay for your passage on a steamship. Take it."

There were tears, there was an embrace so smothering that the two seemed to merge. Then Philip withdrew from the chamber, not looking back.

Only a year before, the city of Pittsburgh had nearly burned to the ground. A fire left unattended under a washwoman's boiling pot had spread to near-by buildings and, whipped up by wind and unquenched by the sparse water dribbling from firemen's mud-clogged hoses, devastated one third of the town. Here and there, one could still see melted glass and charred wood, fragments of collapsed roofs and soot-coated brick.

Philip walked up Diamond Alley, in search of the steamboat office. He kicked aside a section of melted zinc roofing material. Ahead, he saw two men scuffling in the dust. Thinking to avoid the altercation, he crossed to the opposite side where newly constructed buildings cast their shadows on still extant debris. As he passed the men he was startled to recognize the struggling form of Jacob Green.

"What's this?" Philip yelled.

"Mr. Philip, I's telling' him I's a free man. He don't believe me."

Philip pulled the man off Jacob. "That's right," he said. "Leave him alone." The man whirled around to face Philip, reaching into a vest pocket and extracting a long sharp, evil looking knife, Philip reacted immediately to the threat by retrieving his mother's serving spoon from the bag of belongings he carried. He brought the heavy silver spoon hard against the man's skull, knocking him to the ground.

"Quick, Jake, run!" he cried. They ran up the alleyway and down the narrow streets, panting. They reached the canal basin, only to find that the flatboat had gone. "I have to get you away from here, Jake. There are too many bounty hunters in this town." They headed toward the wharf on the Monongahela River side of the city. Several steamboats were moored there. One still had its gangplank extended to the pier. In garishly painted block letters on the wheel housing was its name: "The Messenger."

Isaac eased the flatboat out into the current. The Allegheny joined the Monongahela at the "point" and became the Ohio. It was the first time they had actually had to navigate their craft and they learned quickly that they had a lot to learn. Isaac sat in the stern on top of the latrine house and grasped the long rudder sweep, experimenting with it to turn the boat right or left. John and Dick manned the long sweeps on either side of the flatboat, which were attached by oarlocks to the roof of the cabin. It was necessary to dip these into the river to maintain the angle at which the boat would drift. After precarious practice, during which they nearly sideswiped a keelboat, they began to get the hang of it. Calling back and forth they coordinated their movements to avoid hitting snags and sandbars or venturing too close to shore. It was an exhilarating feeling to fly along the fast moving Ohio. It was frightening to be almost run down by the huge paddleboats that comprised most of the river traffic.

Their seaworthiness was soon put to a test as the river seemed to divide before them. It was, in fact, a huge island, but the fledgling sailors saw two rivers diverging and debated which was the Ohio. "Go left!" "No, go right!" They vacillated until, at the last moment before running aground, Isaac leaned hard on the rudder and took them into the right channel. After this, they sent James to stand on the flat prow of the boat as lookout, a job he appeared to fancy.

Catherine had begun to bake some corn bread, now that she had an ample supply of fine ground corn meal. The cook stove vented through a short chimney on the roof of the cabin, between where John and Dick sat working the side sweeps. The wind took the fumes alternately into the faces of one or the other.

Though they kept a stern vigil for navigating they were not hesitant to observe the flora and fauna of the river valley. "Look there!" John might say upon seeing a snowy egret taking wing. On skirting an island they might see beavers or river otters and scores of leopard frogs splashing into the shallows as they drew near. There was an abundance of fish: long nosed gar, bowfins, sturgeon and pickerel. James watched them over the bow of the boat and yearned to break out the fishing pole and line. Emma held tight to Katy who leaned over the rail watching a red fox disappearing into the brush along the shore. The tall oaks cast long shadows across the river and the sun winked through the branches and between the trunks. This first day on the Ohio was a delight they would look back upon at times when their travels turned sour.

"Mr. Philip, I's thought yo' was gwine to head back east," Jake said as they pushed a large wooden crate along the cargo deck of the Messenger.

"I was, Jake," said Philip.

"Well, I hates at tell yo' but dis boat am gwine west!"

"I know. But I had to get you out of Pittsburgh, didn't I?"

They had scrambled up the gangplank of the steamboat just as it was being drawn aboard. Philip had managed to negotiate passage for them as far as Cincinnati. After that, if they wished to stay on board, they could sign on as crew, the ship's mate had told them. They were relegated to the lower deck, as the upper had its capacity of forty passengers... ones who had paid in cash, rather than in spoons.

The Messenger was a side wheeler, with enclosed paddles on either side. It was essentially a long shallow draft barge carrying a two-level, gaudily painted boxy structure supported by pillars, atop of which sat the pilot house and twin tall smoke stacks that spewed smoke, sparks, and hot ashes. The upper deck was a narrow cabin surrounded by small state rooms which opened on one side into the cabin, and on the opposite, onto an open gallery where passengers could sit and view the passing river bank. The lower deck held the crews' quarters, the poorer passengers, and whatever cargo the ship could contract to haul. The boiler and firebox were open to wind and rain, the crew constantly stoking the fire and greasing the engine.

On their breaks, the crew mingled with the passengers on the lower deck. One of them, a Thomas Hardy by name, struck up a conversation with Philip. "You know, we're famous," he said.

"Famous? How's that?"

"English fellow came through here, oh, three, four years back. A writer, Mr. Dickens he was called."

"I've heard of him. May have read some of his children's stories years ago."

"Well, he wrote about our fine steamboat, he did. Didn't like it much, or America, either, I guess. Anyway, he complained our ships don't look nothing' like real ones... we got no mast or sails and rigging."

Philip laughed. "He never saw a paddle wheeler before, I guess."

"I guess. He was always afeared we'd blow up. Some have, you know."

"Not this one, I hope!"

"Well, he came all the way from Philadelphia by canal boat. We took him over to Cincinnati where, thank God, he got off. All the time he were complainin' 'bout this and that. The washing facilities, for instance. Don't know what they has over in England, but he didn't like them even worse than the food."

"Ah...speaking of food..."

"Chow is at six. Be dried beef, Indian corn, pickles, and lots of corn bread and apple butter."

"Oh good, lots of corn bread," said Philip, having eaten so much of the same during his trip along the canal.

As evening came upon the river, the steamboat chugged and belched its way through the darkness, men with lanterns standing lookout on the bow. Another deckhand stood casting a weighted and knotted line to measure the river's depth—"singing the lead line" it was called. Philip was unaware of the small flatboat moored on the shore which they passed in the night.

CHAPTER 11
A LETTER TO AMELIA

Somewhere on the Ohio River, 22 May, 1846

Dearest Sister,

I hope this finds you well. As I write this, the boat rocks and swings with the stream, so please excuse the smudges and poor penmanship. I shall try to mail this once we get to stop at a large city. We've been on the river for three days now. It is truly beautiful, that is, when it isn't pouring down rain. Even then, with the rattling of drops on the wooden roof above me, there is a sense of belonging to this great natural wilderness through which we journey. We float through a sort of dream world where there are no people, only giant trees and the rushing of the current. Sometimes I feel as if the boat could lift and fly away!

Isaac and the boys must man the sweeps even in inclement weather. Luckily, it hasn't stormed much. The greatest danger comes from the large river boats that charge up and down the river without so much as a care for flatboats being slower and in the way. We hug the shore line when we hear the splashing of their paddle wheels and the snorting of their engines. People on the galleries sometimes point and jeer at us as they go by. Some people are thoughtless that way.

We've encountered a few of our fellow bargemen, in flatboats sometimes twice the size of our own, and keelboats, which are propelled by men with long sticks walking along the sides. A pirogue or a canoe may be seen with fishermen, or boys with crude fishing poles made from willow branches, as we drift past log cabins set back along the banks, though these are few. There is an occasional exchange between us and these pioneers, as they have built out short piers on which they stand and "Hal-loo," to us. More cordial than the steamboat passengers! They too, have come from back east to make a new life in West Virginia or Ohio, and I suppose, farther a field, as we do.

Much of the activity on the river is for purposes of commerce, with barges and flatboats loaded with livestock and produce. But we have seen families like ours, struggling, as we do, with this new enterprise of running a boat. How ungainly it is! A big square-nosed raft that's likely to run aground before one can turn it. Indeed, we've seen wrecked boats on the sand bars and snags near the islands. Plenty of them! It gives us a caution and a chill to anticipate the prospect of striking a tree trunk or a rock that pokes out of the shallows. But we persevere and with God's help we will reach Illinois in a few weeks more.

I have to tell you that Philip left us at Pittsburgh to come home. By the time you get this letter he should be there, and I trust he will bring you news of us. I was saddened to have him leave, but as Isaac says, he is a grown man and must make his own decisions. I don't think he quite has the courage or the willingness to embrace adventure that his father has. In a way, I wish it were the reverse, and we had stayed home. You know, we talked long hours of this. But I must follow my husband, no matter what.

There are times when I find myself alone in the cabin, the girls out playing on the deck, that I cry a little. I can't help myself and I don't let anyone see my despondency. I have to be brave and act as if everything is normal and good, for if the little ones become afraid, it will tear us all apart, I feel. Emma has been a great help to me, watching over little Katy like she has. She would rather be playing at games with her older sisters, I am sure. But there is a bond between her and Katy. I think it makes her feel important— like a "little mother," and that is just what she is, for I have my own work cut out for me.

And we had passenger—a black man, a runaway slave, according to Isaac, who hid on the boat. A man came to try to capture him but Philip and Dick threw him overboard! It was exciting and a little scary! I guess we're part of that Underground Railroad now. The man left us at Pittsburgh where Philip got off. I wish him well and hope he gets to

Canada without further problems.

Cooking on a small cast iron stove in close quarters is nothing I would recommend. I tried baking bread, but there isn't an oven, and I have only an iron kettle with a lid which takes forever to get hot. It can be done that way, I know, but the boys complain that the cabin gets too hot. They are threatening to move my kitchen outdoors—we see other flatboats with this arrangement, but they have only a firepit open to the wind. I've put my foot down. I can do cornbread and types of biscuits but no cakes or pies or real loaves. We get some pork or chicken when we dock at a good sized town. These are getting far between. I know Isaac would love it if I could rustle up a little scrapple for him, but it's so complicated and takes too long to cook. James has tried fishing but the boat moves too fast and Isaac will not stop for long. Yesterday, he did haul in three Pikes when we tied up for the evening. These we promptly cleaned and fried in some bacon fat I managed to save.

We sleep inside the cabin in bunks, four on each side and two in the middle. The boys sometimes like to sleep out on the deck in the cool night with a little fagot smoldering in a bucket to smoke off the mosquitoes. I insisted on bringing our copper bathtub which we built a little outhouse and bathhouse for at the rear of the boat. Our usual Saturday night bathing has gone for naught, though, as the boys prefer to drop over the side of the boat and splash around in the muddy shallows. So much more warm water for us! Little Katy is probably the only one of us that likes the bath, even though the water is getting cold by the time she gets into it.

Your son, Dick, has been a pleasure to have among us. Now with Philip gone, he somewhat occupies the role of eldest son, although John should be appointed to this. But John is so quiet, now. I think he misses his older brother as much as I do. Dick helps with the sweeps and what ever day to day chores there are: cleaning fallen leaves and branches from the deck, securing the barrels, finding fire wood. I look forward to the time, after we arrive in Illinois, when Dick finds you farmland next to wherever we end up and you can join us. He is, as you can imagine, desirous of returning home and marrying Sara Ann. He says to me,

"Auntie Catherine, I'm love sick!" When he saw that Philip had gone home, I think he was very envious.

I never told you this, and I haven't told Isaac, but I'm also expecting a child! Yours and mine are both due in October, if all goes well. I know I should have told you before this, but I was afraid you would have too much influence on me and make me oppose the trip west. Isaac would have waited and lost the opportunity to go at all, I firmly believe. I hope you can forgive me not confiding in you, but I am a weak woman and I couldn't stand up between two opposite forces such as you and Isaac are.

I always looked up to you as my older sister and you always took good care of me. When Daddy got mad because I turned loose the chickens or came home covered in mud you always defended me. Now you must understand that you have so much sway over me it would conflict with my duty toward Isaac. But now I am on the river, headed for a new home!

Oddly, the thing I miss the most is my garden. The snap dragons would be in bloom now. The flocks and the azaleas and the corn flowers—add so much color to our lives! To have trumpet flowers climbing a trellis! And to be able to pull up a carrot or a turnip for a stew! Living on a boat does have its drawbacks! I remember once walking into town from the valley. I thought it was such a distance I would die before I got there. Now, what I would give just to walk down a dirt road for some miles and feel the solid earth beneath my feet!

But I have my children, all but Philip, I mean. John is solid as ever. Dutiful toward his father. And Will—Will is my darling! He always has a kind and encouraging word to say to me when I get a bit down. And he dotes on James. James—when will he ever settle down? He is like a wild animal sometimes, running off on his own if we tie up at an island for wood! But his energy is intoxicating. He is a joy and a heartache at the same time! Mary Jane, now there's a strange one. She's a bit of a tomboy and she goes with James on a rampage, then is sweet as fresh honey—her smile can melt you! Elizabeth, poor Elizabeth is a middle child, of sorts. Too young to go with the older ones and too old to be saddled with Emma and Katy. She likes reading books, that one. She's far cleverer than I and perhaps the rest of us for that matter. But you know all this. I just feel, if I had you here to talk all these things over with, my world would be a different place.

I should ask you for news of the valley and the folks. I don't know how you could reach me, though. Better to wait until we're settled and have some kind of an address—other than this floating disaster! I'll go now, and remember, you are in my thoughts, you and yours.

Your loving sister, Catherine

CHAPTER 12
ALONG THE BANKS OF THE O-HI-O

Cincinnati, Ohio, 22 May, 1846

The steam powered side wheeler, Messenger, reached Cincinnati in only three days, stopping briefly at Wheeling in the Commonwealth of Virginia to take on cargo and passengers. Here it was that Philip would get his first look at the upper deck of the steamboat. They had docked at the large wharf at Wheeling, where the building of flatboats, keelboats, and steamboats had become a major industry. Philip and Jacob watched as Thomas Hardy and his crewmates rolled barrels up the gangplank and maneuvered heavy crates onto the Messenger. With the deck crew thus occupied, Philip climbed the narrow stairway to the upper galleries and entered the salon of the Texas deck, as this upper story was called.

Inside the salon, a narrow hall with a high ceiling ran the length of the Texas deck. There was a long wooden table surrounded by velvet covered chairs on which small plates of food were arrayed. A rich, ornate carpet graced the floor and crystal chandeliers hung from the ceiling at intervals, their dangling prisms casting rainbow patterns against gilded pillars. Fanciful oil paintings ineptly imitating Flemish landscapes decorated the stateroom doors. There was a gentlemen's bar at one end, at which several men in shirt sleeves leaned, one foot propped upon a brass rail. The other end of the hall was apparently reserved for ladies, with chairs and a couch upholstered in striped fabric and a jardinière filled with yellow daffodils. Women in fashionable dress lounged or stood engaged in conversation as Philip made his way to the bar end of the salon.

At a gaming table, three men, again coatless, played a

card game which, owning to the stacks of red, white and blue chips in front of them, Philip deemed to be poker. Cigars issued wisps of smoke, fragrant, but not able to overcome the odor of wood smoke that permeated the boat from its boiler room below. Glasses half filled with amber liquid left rings on the green felt of the table and burn marks from idle cigars decorated the table's edge.

"Boy," uttered one of the gamblers, "get me another Scotch!"

"I'm sorry, sir," answered Philip, "I don't work here."

"What are you doing here then?" asked the man.

"Just observing. I may decide to travel first class some day. Need to see if it's worth the extra money."

"Steward!" yelled the man. "Get this riff raff out of here." But the steward was no where to be seen—all the better for Philip, who crept out a door onto a balcony at the foredeck.

Here was an enthralling view of the bustling city of Wheeling. A dozen steamboats docked at her wharves. A busy freight and rail yard where steam locomotives belched dark clouds of smoke into the cloudless sky was spread out before him. Other vast pillars of smoke rose from the tall stacks of foundries behind the rail yard. Like other river towns that had experienced a boom in commerce, houses of log and board were intermixed with grand edifices of brick; the hovels of the working classes nestled beside residences of the newly wealthy. Not a sprawling metropolis like Pittsburgh, Wheeling still impressed, especially if you were from German Valley, Pennsylvania. As Philip looked out on this vista, the boat whistle suddenly squealed. The ship's mate climbed down a ladder from the pilot house above to stand next to Philip on the balcony.

"Do you have a stateroom?" he quizzed.

"No, I do not."

"Oh, I recognize you. You're the kid with the silver spoon. You shouldn't be up here."

"I gathered as much from what a fellow in there said to me, only not in as nice terms as you use."

"They pay well to be exclusive. Makes 'em feel important. Say, I did offer to take you and your friend on as crew, didn't I?"

"Yes, sir, you did. That was very helpful."

"You're a nice looking kid. Maybe I'll put you in the salon, carrying drinks and waiting on the big table at dinner."

"No thanks. I'd probably get mad and punch somebody."

"How about your friend, the colored man? He'd certainly know how to act."

"What makes you say that?"

"I think we both know why I say that. Just tell your friend, when we get to Kentucky, to stay on the Ohio side of the ship."

Philip thought this over as he descended a stairway and entered the engine area. Heat from the open fires was stifling. The boilers were getting up a good head of steam and a second whistle announced the ship's imminent departure. With wheezes and coughs, sputters and groans, the pistons pumped and safety valves hissed. An engineer threw a lever to engage the drive shaft and the great water wheels began to turn. The Messenger backed slowly away from the wharf and into the river channel. Throwing the lever again reversed the direction of the crankshaft and the boat surged forward down the mighty Ohio.

As they rolled down the river some of the deck crew, black men now idle after having loaded sugar and sundries, wool and whiskey, potatoes, lard and bees' wax, broke into song:

> De smoke goes up and de ingine roars
> And de wheel goes round and round,
> So fair you well! for I'll take a little ride
> When de river boat comes down.
> I'll work all night in de wind and storm,
> I'll work all day in de rain,
> Till I find myself on de levy dock
> In New Orleans again.

They had passed Sistersville and Newport that first day out from Pittsburgh. Bellville, Ravenswood, Apple Grove and Proctorville, the second. High bluffs could be seen past the bottom land lining the river banks. The river meandered and coiled like a monstrous snake and split into channels around hundreds of islands, big and small, all thickly wooded. Philip saw smaller boats headed eastward, struggling against the current. The keelboats, propelled by manpower, had to be towed by ropes from the shore. Men would sometime loop the ropes around tree trunks for extra leverage. This was called "bushwhacking," Thomas Hardy told Philip.

As they neared Cincinnati on the third day, Philip and Jacob Green stood at the stern rail, watching the froth of the steamboat's wake. Philip knew they had a decision to make: stay with the boat and sign on as crew, or land at Cincinnati where Philip might find passage eastward to return home while Jacob continued his trek to Canada. A third possibility occurred to Philip. If he waited at Cincinnati and watched the river vigilantly, he might spot his family's flatboat which was surely still down river traveling more slowly. Homesickness for the German Valley fought against his need to again be surrounded by brothers and sisters, to see his father and mother, to join with them, stalwart and dauntless in their valiant undertaking. It was risky to wait for the flatboat, as he might miss seeing it, or they might pass along the opposite side of the river. Might they not stop at the famous city for supplies? Could he sit alone on the wharf and watch for as long as it might take?

"What will you do?" Philip asked Jacob.

"Well, Suh, I's 'spect my best bet be to sign on dis boat and go all the ways to St. Louis. That's close to Canada, ain't it?"

"Perhaps that's the best thing for you to do, Jake. I believe there are sympathetic people on this boat. Ask Tom Hardy, he'll know. St. Louis could be dangerous for you."

"I knows it. Ain't you comin' too?"

"Jake, I will wait at Cincinnati for my family to arrive and rejoin them. It's a funny thing. I wanted to be my own man, not all the time doing what my father expected me to do. I was so intent on breaking that bond that I was willing to separate myself from my family, the people I most care about in the world. I'm faced again with a choice, and...I understand now what I really want."

"I'll be missin' yo', Mr. Philip."

"And I, you, Jake. I wish you luck. It seems I'm always saying goodbye on this trip!"

Paddle wheelers, barges with their tow boats, and all manner of packet boats were lined up along the Cincinnati waterfront and must have looked to an observer on Kentucky side of the river as if a extravagantly decorated aquatic circus train had pulled along side. The Messenger found a space between The Telegraph and The Ohio Belle and docked. Philip, his meager belongings in a rucksack slung over his shoulder, scrambled down the gangplank and onto the shore.

"Welcome to Porkopolis," someone said. Pens filled with snorting hogs waiting to be loaded onto river boats lined the waterfront just upriver from where they had docked. The smell was overpowering: Philip had never seen so many animals in one place nor had he realized just how malodorous their intensified aroma could be. He turned and walked rapidly up the hill and down a city street. His plan to wait for the flatboat had one inescapable flaw: He had no money.

He wandered up East Front street looking at notices posted in windows. One announced a *"Debate On Slavery, To Be Held The Second, Third and Sixth This Month, Upon The Question, Is Slave-holding In Itself Sinful? And The Relation Between Slave And Master A Sinful Relationship?"* Others announced a position for a clerk to travel with the steamboat, Schuykill, and ship's mate for the Mary Stevens. When he reached Cassilly's Row, where a number of steamship companies had their offices, an idea crept into his consciousness. If he could get a job unloading boats at the wharf, he could earn money and keep a lookout for his family at the same time. He peered through the smoke stained windows of the offices of Irwin and Foster, Agents. It appeared to be a booking agency. Stealing up his nerve, Philip entered.

He was asked to wait while the clerk sent for his boss, a Mr. Foster. He sat on a hard bench and began humming one of the songs he had heard while on the Messenger: "O de smoke goes up and de ingine roars, and de wheel goes round and round," unconsciously singing the words in a soft voice. A young man entered from an inner office. Slender, with large, dark brown eyes and an amiable smile, he introduced himself as Mr. Stephen Foster, head clerk and brother of Mr. Dunning Foster, one of the owners. "What was that song you were singing?" he inquired.

"Oh, it's one the colored folk sing on the riverboats," answered Philip. "I've heard many more. And plantation songs as well." He thought of the songs Jacob Green had taught them.

"I'd like to hear some more," said Mr. Foster.

Philip began his new career as a roustabout on the wharves of Cincinnati, hired out by Irwin and Foster on an adjunct basis. He was able to watch the river but was discouraged to notice that the flatboat traffic kept to the Kentucky side so as to avoid the larger boats. It would be some days, he knew, before Isaac's boat would pass by, so he worked hard to earn adequate money to support himself for a few weeks, intending to cross the river where he could better see the features of those who piloted flatboats down the Ohio. He talked often with his employer, Mr. Foster, who quizzed him about the songs he knew and he explained to him his goal of reuniting with his family. It was understood his tenure at Irwin and Foster would be brief, having an alternate ambition, something, apparently, with which Stephen Foster could identify.

One day, Foster pulled Philip aside and said he wanted him to listen to a song he was writing for his social club. A quartet formed by the men of the club, he explained, performed at ice cream socials and liked to do minstrel songs. Did it sound like an authentic negro song, Foster wanted to know. He sang:

> It rain'd all night
> De day I lef
> De wedder it was dry
> De sun so hot,
> I froze to death
> Amanda, don' you cry
>
> Oh! Amanda,
> Oh don' you cry for me
> For I come from Alabamy

Widda trumpet on my knee

"What do you think?" Foster asked. "Would the darkies sing like that?"

"Well, it needs a little work, but I sort of liked it. I don't know about the girl's name, 'Amanda,' though. How about something like...Sara, or...Susan?"

"Susan? Hm...well, it needs to be three syllables to fit the rhythm."

"How about Susannah? And...shouldn't he be playing, say, a fiddle, or a banjo?"

"Banjo. Yes. I like that."

"Do you have any more verses?"

"I thought the singer would be on the way to New Orleans to see his girl. Something like 'I saw her comin' down the hill.... I don't know, I might change the melody a little too."

"I like that kind of polka beat."

"Well thanks. You'd better get back down to the wharf now. I hope the job is going well?"

"It's okay. I like hard work. Keeps me fit. Some of the fellows have good stories to tell, as well."

"You'll have to tell me some. Might make good song lyrics."

CHAPTER 13
EMMA IN PERIL

Ohio River near Portsmouth, Ohio, 1 June, 1846

They'd been drifting for two weeks since leaving Pittsburgh. The current carried them only about 2 miles per hour. Snags and sandbars slowed them down as they maneuvered around them. A peaceful, gently flowing river, the Ohio wasn't ready to display the fury of tumbling white water she was capable of producing—that would come much later. Now she was placid, tranquil, and slow. Isaac's estimate of one month of travel was being dashed.

Still, they'd become accustomed to life on the water. The close quarters of the flatboat irked, but they beached at night and hiked along the bottom lands, the children finding odd shaped rocks, and the older boys looking to shoot a rabbit or squirrel or perhaps a wild turkey with Isaac's Springfield flintlock musket. For years, Philip and John had urged Isaac to have the smooth bored weapon rifled and converted to the new percussion cap system, but Isaac failed to see the need. You didn't need to fire minié balls at rabbits, and, if all you did was to scare the varmints away from your garden, well, that was sufficient.

The old muzzle-loader looked as if it hadn't seen action since the War of 1812, although it was a Model 1835. It took a priming charge, a black powder packet, wadding, a 69 caliper musket ball and more wadding, all of which were loaded through the barrel and pushed tightly into place by a ramrod. It was easy to see why the rabbit got away if the first ball missed. John carried the musket cradled in one arm and trudged as quietly as he was able through the dense brush. So far, no game had presented itself.

The hunting party consisted of John, Will and James

and it was James who plunged ahead, attempting to flush out some quarry or other. It was not a practical stratagem, however, as John certainly did not want to mistake James for a rabbit.

"James! Get back here!" he called.

"Aw... " said James as his head appeared from behind a blackberry bush. "Can I carry the gun now?"

"No you can't. I don't want to be shot accidentally or otherwise!"

"Bet I could shoot me a bear," said James, picking up a long stick and brandishing it. "Bang! Bang!"

"Well, whatever may have been here has been scared away, you can be sure of that."

"James," said Will, "you are a nuisance and a nincompoop!"

"It will be getting dark soon," said John. "We'd better start back. You know, it's funny we haven't seen so much as a squirrel. Something's scaring the game away."

They had stopped for the evening at a bend in the Ohio where the river turned due west in its incessant meandering. As the sun hung above the horizon, perhaps hesitant to retire for the night, it set the river on fire with golden undulations and splatters of silvery sparks. Along the banks under the towering trees, the shadows were deeper and the way precarious. The boys walked along the rocks and sand by the river's edge, to avoid the fallen branches that seemed determined to trip the unwary.

"Well, I don't like squirrel anyway," said James.

"You like rabbit, don't you?" asked Will.

"Maybe in a stew, I guess. I like beef better."

"I don't think we're likely to shoot a cow along the river," joked Will.

"Maybe a buffalo or a rhinoceros," added John to further provoke his little brother.

"I still want to shoot a bear," replied James, sensing he was being made fun of but only taking the bait on his own terms.

"Maybe you'll get the chance someday."

Elizabeth, Emma and Katy were also down river from the flatboat, occupied with building imaginary castles on the sandy embankment. Emma would establish an elaborate construction of rocks and Katy would immediately demolish it, expressing her amusement with gleeful whooping. After a time, Emma grew weary of this one-sided game, and, as Elizabeth was present to watch over Katy, felt it her privilege, in fact, her duty, to abandon her charge and indulge her adventurous spirit with a short expedition. And so she wandered off exploring the riverside.

"Don't go too far," warned Elizabeth.

Emma was walking directly into the blooming glow of the setting sun and its brilliance mesmerized her. The dark outlines of the trees formed strange shapes that teased her imagination, becoming colossal giants and behemoths from fabled antiquity. Flames seemed to flare up where the flow of the river rippled over a submerged boulder. It was a fantasy world fraught with dangers that thrilled the girl, enticed her to venture a bit further into unguarded territory. She could imagine that the protruding limbs of nearby trees were arms that reached out for her. She could visualize the twisted twigs that lay on the ground before her as serpents, coiled and hissing a warning to her: don't advance toward me!

Suddenly, Emma's vision cleared and she found herself staring into the ugly features of a real snake—a timber rattler, coiled, tongue darting in and out, and rattles vibrating with an eerie sound that made her feel like a block of ice was sliding down her back. She stood rigid and breathless. It wasn't that she knew she shouldn't make a sudden move, she simply froze. The snake swayed, its head elevated, its mouth a crimson crescent flecked with foam. The child and the snake were locked in a deadly stare, each seeming to challenge the other to move first.

"Where is Emma?" Catherine asked as Elizabeth hefted Katy up and unto the flatboat.

"Oh, she took off. I told her not to go far."

"You shouldn't have let her wander off alone!"

"But, Mother, I had to watch Katy. That's Emma's job, anyway. I couldn't watch them both."

"It's all our jobs to take care of each other. Now I'll worry sick until Emma returns."

"Would you like me to go fetch her?" asked Dick Cornelius.

"Give her a few more minutes, then, maybe you should do that, Dick. Thank you."

"Now where did James go?" said John, turning around.

"He was right here a minute ago," answered Will. "He's off on his own again. He's incorrigible!"

"We'll have to wait or go looking for him. It's going to get really dark soon, and I don't want to be walking along the bank in the dark."

There was a rustling in the bushes and suddenly James emerged, covered in burrs and prickers.

"Ouch!" he cried.

"Bear get ya?" asked Will.

"Very funny. I got a little lost."

"Well, stay with us, dang it!" admonished John.

Emma stared at the snake. The snake stared at Emma. The twitching of its rattles seemed deafeningly loud. Emma began to shake. Could the snake smell her fear, she wondered. Its tongue flipped up and down as if in answer to her thoughts. It arched in preparation for the strike, scales glistening in the sun's diminishing glow. All at once a new sound caught Emma's attention. From the brush came what appeared to be a ball of fur with teeth and claws. Emma saw a small dog rushing toward the snake, howling. Now she feared for the animal as much as for herself. The snake, confused by the presence of two antagonists, gave up its position and slithered away into the woods.

"Oh, doggie!" cried Emma. "Why, you're just a puppy, aren't you? What are you doing here?"

She moved toward the dog, grateful it had scared away the snake. She wanted to hug the animal, hold it, in part to quell the shaking of her own body, in part to express a love she instantly felt for it. There was something about the dog, though, something exceedingly wild. The animal backed away from her, as if it had never before seen a human. It growled but did not bark. Strange, thought Emma, a dog that doesn't bark. As she tried to coax the pup to allow her to approach, something large crashed out of the woods.

Between her and the pup that she had thought was a dog, now stood the snarling, drooling form of its mother, a she-wolf, intent on protecting her offspring. The wolf crouched, ready to spring.

As John, Will and James lumbered along the shoreline they could see Emma in the distance. Suddenly the figure of a timber wolf leaped from the woods and confronted the girl. They began to run. As they neared the scene, the wolf turned toward them. Its teeth bared, the wolf menaced the three new humans that now threatened its pup. John, terrified, raised the flintlock to his shoulder and pulled back the lever to cock the weapon. The wolf came forward, slowly at first, then gaining momentum. As it sprang John fired. At point blank range the ball smashed into the animal's brain, killing it instantly. It fell in a heap at John's feet.

"Oh, God!" John cried.

They all stood motionless, fixed in disbelief. The pup was sniffing at his mother's still warm corpse, whining. Emma came to the pup and now was able to encircle it in her arms. The wolf pup, instead of struggling, licked the girl's face. John would later remember the moment as one of the most bizarre he had ever experienced.

"What do we do with the pup?" asked Will.

"I don't know, leave it, I guess," John answered.

"It'll die. With no mother."

"Oh, I want to take it," said Emma. "It will be my puppy. Please?"

"Emma, it isn't a dog. It's a wolf. What happens when it grows up?"

"I'll take care of it and it'll think it's a dog."

"I have heard," offered Will, "of people raising wolves as dogs. If you take them out of the wild you can domesticate them."

"You're going to explain this to Father, then?"

At the flatboat, Catherine was beside herself with worry and sent Dick out to find Emma. When he met the group he was surprised to see Emma carrying a small dog in her arms. Upon hearing the whole story of the snake and the wolf, a story he was requested not to repeat in its entirety, Dick looked at the wolf pup and shook his head.

"What are you going to feed it?" Dick asked Emma.

"Maybe we could shoot some squirrels," laughed James.

"Shut up," said Will.

"What will you name it," asked John, now more sympathetic toward the girl's request to keep the wolf pup.

"Well, he saved me from the snake. Like a knight in shining armor. And look, there's a silver mark on his forehead—like a lightning bolt. I'll call him 'Lancelot.'"

The following morning they set off down the river, passing the town of Portsmouth. Will and Dick manned the side sweeps and Isaac was at the rear sweep as usual. James was at his post at the bow of the boat, whittling a piece of cottonwood with a rusty old bowie knife. John sat on a box with Emma playing Jacks at his feet. Lancelot was curled up next to Emma, his chin resting on her lap. There was an unusually cool nip in the early morning air, something left over from yesterday's chilly drama, John supposed. Emma looked up at her brother, sadness in her eyes.

"I wish you hadn't killed Lancelot's mommy," she said.

"I wish that too, Em, only if I hadn't of fired, I might not be here today."

"And Lancelot might not be my doggie, is that right?"

"That's right. And just remember, Lancelot *is* a dog. That's what we told Mother."

"I know. I don't think Papa believed us, though."

There was a loud thump and the boat stopped dead in the water. Will scrambled up to look over the bow and saw that they had struck a large boulder.

"James! Why aren't you watching where we're going?" he called.

James leaped over prow of the flatboat onto the rock. "Look!" he said. "It's covered with inscriptions. Just like the Standing Stone back home!"

Indeed it was. There were names and dates and a curious drawing that looked like a smiling face. "Look at this face somebody carved!"

"That," said Will, "could be an Indian sign. The first

Standing Stone was supposed to be covered with Indian signs like that. Better get back up here. We have to back off this rock."

"No wait. Just a minute. I have to do something." And James began dragging the rusty knife to and fro across the surface of the rock. "Just one more second!"

They pushed off from the rock and floated freely once more down the mighty Ohio, leaving behind them a new inscription on the great boulder that the people of Portsmouth called their "Indian Head Rock." It read, "John Grosh killed a wolf here, 1846."

CHAPTER 14
REUNION

Approaching Cincinnati, Ohio, 6 June, 1846

Lancelot was settling in, learning how to be a dog. He hadn't warmed up to the flatboat right away, but diligent sniffing and exploring had convinced him that there was nothing to fear and that here was an abundance of new things to consider. He could chew on boxes, lift his leg on barrels and stand on his hind legs to look over the side of the flatboat as it drifted lazily down the river. He liked the flavor of the dried beef jerky he was offered, but he wasn't too keen on the cornbread. He missed being able to run down bull frogs along the river bank, but he found a family of field mice living among the boxes and crates and harried them as only a young wolf pup can.

These two-legged creatures were a strange lot. The littlest one liked to tussle and poke at him, playing, the way he and his littermates had once done. A few gentle nips established the limits of the game but sometimes resulted in the little one making an annoying noise—something like howling, but different. The bigger ones would then intervene and make other noises, something like the scolding growl his mother used to make, but different. It was confusing.

One by one his littermates had left, leaving him the only pup. Then his mother had gone to sleep and wouldn't wake up and he was alone, except for these two-legs. The one that had held him, he liked her best of all. The bigger ones didn't pay him as much attention. In the evenings they would get off the floating island and play in the woods. He would run and they would call him, coax him with food, and he would return to ride on the island with them again.

He was beginning to understand what some of the strange sounds they made meant. "Food" was his favorite. "No," his least favorite. "Lancelot," a very strange sound, meant a number of things: that he should run back to them, that he was about to be petted or that "Food" was present, or that the bad sound, "No," would follow.

One of the bigger two-legs that he also liked was the one that sat at the front of the floating island. That one would scratch him behind the ears and make soft sounds that soothed and calmed him. He learned how to climb the ladder to the top deck and jump down on the prow where James was keeping a vigil against rocks and snags. Together they would survey the watery scene in front of them, watching aquatic birds diving for fish or marveling at the occasional uprooted tree that drifted along side. The large river boats frightened him. He'd heard their puffing and whistling before, of course, but never this close. James would stroke the back of his neck when he cowered, and the fear would pass.

It was early morning and a thick mist was rising from the river making it difficult to see more than a few feet ahead. James and Lancelot were perched on the bow of the flatboat, James shouting back if he observed a snag or sandbar. As the mist gradually dissipated he could make out the hazy shapes of buildings and large boats.

"Large city ahead on the left," he called. "Big ships. Better keep to the right bank."

Isaac pulled on the rear sweep and John, manning the left side sweep, began rowing. Too murky and indistinct to gauge the distance to shore, the flatboat slammed into a sandbar and hung there like a beached whale. "Well," said John, "we've arrived."

"Yes, but where?" asked Dick.

"I think we're back in Huntingdon," said James, chuckling to himself.

"What do you mean?"

"Look!" James pointed to shore where they could just barely make out a long sliver of a shape that thrust upward from the top of a low bluff. "It looks like we're back at the Standing Stone!"

And there it was, the slender odalisque that graced the hilltop in Huntingdon, that early pioneers had carved their names and dates upon and that Isaac had so admired— somehow magically transported to this spot. It sat gleaming in the rays of a rising sun that tried desperately to burn away the gloom of the misty morning. But how could that be?

"I have to see this," said James. And with that he jumped from the prow of the flatboat into the shallows and waded to shore with Lancelot at his heels. The wolf pup shook the water from his fur and followed James as he scrambled up the bluff toward whatever the thing was that just couldn't be there. When they reached it his hand went instinctively to its surface as he'd seen his father do many times at the Standing Stone—the real one. For this was bogus. It wasn't even stone, it was a piece of wood, cleverly crafted and erected to imitate the monument they had left behind so many days and weeks and river and canal miles ago. But by who? And why?

"Pretty good replica, don't you think," a voice said. Lancelot growled and James spun around.

"Philip! Is it you?"

"In the flesh." Philip hugged his brother. "And who might this be?" he said, indicating the wolf pup.

"Oh, this is Lancelot. He's our... dog. Emma brought him aboard. A stray she picked up."

"That's good. Where is the boat? I've been waiting for you all for quite a long time. We'll have some catching up to be doing, I think."

"I knew I'd never see you," Philip said, "and so I had to make you see me. The only thing I could think of you'd recognize was the Standing Stone. I was sure you'd investigate."

"You're lucky we saw it at all in that mist."

"Well, I got a piece of wood and painted it white and placed up on that bluff. I've been camping up there for a week now. My money was running out."

Catherine fairly cried out for joy when she saw Philip climbing over the side of the flatboat. "Philip... Philip!" was all she could say, tears welling up in her eyes. She drew him to her, throwing her arms around him and he returned her loving embrace ecstatically. Mother and son thus reunited, Philip now turned to Isaac saying, "Father, thank you for letting me go on my own. Now I am returned." Perhaps Isaac thought of the bible tale of the prodigal son, perhaps not. At any rate, he was elated, relieved, and also a bit teary-eyed. The girls were next to embrace Philip, running to him and nearly knocking him over. John, Will, and Dick were less raucous in their welcome, yet hugged Philip until he had to say, "Stop!"

While they waited for the mist to burn off, Philip told them the story of how he and Jacob had escaped from the bounty hunter and traveled by side wheeler to Cincinnati. How Jacob had stayed on the boat and he had gotten a job working on the river front. James and Mary Jane asked him many questions about life in the big city. "Wait 'til we stop for the evening," Philip said, "and I'll tell you all about that." And Philip was eager to hear how they had fared on the river in the small boat. How they had come to be traveling with a small... dog.

They pulled and pushed and finally dislodged the boat from the sand bar. The sun had won its battle with the mist and they saw the spectacular panorama of the waterfront of Cincinnati with the rows of paddle wheelers hugging its wharves. The city sat cradled in a horseshoe bend of the river; buildings as tall as three or four stories and the thin spires of churches reaching toward the now bluing sky. They commenced drifting and paddling and their journey began anew.

They started to notice more and more flatboats moored along the banks and landings of small river towns. As they neared a group of perhaps six or seven boats lashed together, they saw that this was a floating city of houses and shops built from flatboats and rafts of every size and description. Signs announced a barber shop, a blacksmith's shop, produce and dry goods stores and several dram shops. At a "flatboat city" on the Kentucky side there were advertisements for something called "moonshine" in earthen jugs. Isaac, although not a teetotaler, didn't partake of spirits in excess nor did he approve of those who did. He was true to his Brethren upbringing in this regard.

In fact, his grandfather, Christopher, had been in the ministry back in Lancaster County. His own father, Philip, was a charter member of the Brethren Church back in Huntingdon.

They explored the flatboat city and found the prices outrageous and the produce of dubious quality. Meat, however, could be obtained very fresh, that is, if you were willing to butcher your own hog or wring the neck of your own chicken. Catherine perused the poultry, a half dozen skinny pullets in cages. She selected three of these for she intended to prepare a nice meal for Philip's homecoming. Lancelot was beside himself when Catherine brought the chickens onto the boat, leaping and jumping and hearing a lot of the "No!" word. He soon found himself confined to the cabin, the door barricaded with Isaac's rocker.

Catherine retrieved a small hatchet from the tool box and promptly dispatched the chickens whose now headless bodies ran wildly along the deck, flopped and fell, spattering blood everywhere. Mary Jane, Elizabeth and Emma were set to task of plucking feathers, which they threw overboard to float along side of the slow moving boat. If that dog would behave himself, Catherine thought to herself, he might get the heads and the legs. She wrapped the freshly plucked chickens in paper and placed them in one of the barrels where sawdust and wood shavings would keep them from the heat of the day and began to plan her meal: chicken parts rolled in flour and fried in an iron skillet in some good lard, dried corn that could be resuscitated and boiled, and, of course, corn bread and molasses.

"I stayed," began Philip, once the evening meal had been consumed and the family had arranged themselves in a semicircle around him, "in what they called a 'workmen's hotel.' It was a single room with a dozen or so beds in little cubicles formed by hanging canvas sheets over ropes. There was one bathroom, down the hall, and we all used it. It was cheap, though. And all you did there was sleep—some mornings I'd wake up covered with bites that itched like the dickens. We took meals out on the pier, where there were food venders—again, cheap. It was the only way to save money.

"Roustabout work on the docks was hard—we worked from dawn 'til dusk. Sometimes there were confrontations with the deckhands from the big steamboats, especially our blacks. You see, we were paid better. And some of the other roustabouts were from across the river in Kentucky where they still have slaves and, you know, they didn't like the fact that the blacks on the boats were free men. Mostly, though, it was just herding pigs or hauling crates. Being a laborer isn't all that bad, I guess. It keeps you healthy.

"One night I heard about a circus that was in town. I knew they sometimes hired locals to help strike the tents and so forth, so I went up to the parade grounds where the circus was to see what I could see. It wasn't much, just a side show and a small tent. No elephants or camels or anything. But I wasn't there to see a show, just to get some work. One thing that was fascinating though, they had these little people, midgets, they're called. Tiny, perfectly proportioned little men and women, six of them. At first I thought they were children, but the men smoked cigars and were dressed...well, the women, they were all dolled up like dance hall dames.

"Anyway, the city of Cincinnati has this peace keeping force that are called the night watch. They roam the streets at night carrying heavy sticks called billy clubs, which they will bring down upon the head of anyone creating a ruckus. It so happened that as I was walking along the rows of side show tents I saw a man being held up at knife point by a thug. There was a shrill whistle and a night watchman appeared, brandishing his billy. The thug saw this and went for him with the knife. Before I could call for more help or intervene myself, which wouldn't have been wise, the watchman was stabbed and fell to the ground holding his stomach. I ran into one of the tents and yelled, "Murder!" As you can imagine, a throng of people poured out onto the midway, but by that time, the killer had fled and the watchman was lying in a pool of blood, barely conscious.

"I don't know if he died or not. They took him away in a horse cart, I suppose to a hospital. I decided to stick with my job on the docks after that."

"Wow!" said James. "That's some story!"

"I knew you'd like it, Jimmy. But there's more. I met an old fellow working on the docks named Bill Strunk. He'd been working on the river since time began, I guess. He had stories!"

"Indians?"

"No, no Indians as I remember. But he did tell me a story once about river pirates."

"Pirates!"

"Wait 'til you hear this," Philip said, settling back against a barrel. Lancelot lay beside him, his chin resting on Philip's lap...a conquest of sorts. Philip stroked the wolf pup's back and began his story.

CHAPTER 15
RIVER PIRATES

The wharf at Cincinnati, Ohio, 28 May, 1846:
Bill Strunk's story

You just sit yourself down, young fella, and let ol' Bill Strunk entertain ya while ya rest. I see these other roustabouts here are doomed to follow the river life, but not you, son. You've got that gleam in yer eye that tells me you'll be movin' on soon. Just so's you know about it, I'll tell you a tale about this grand old river—and her dangers.

Why, I wasn't no more older than you are right now. I was working on a Kentucky boat, that's a big flatboat, you know, and we was hauling pigs we got right here in Porkopolis down to New Orleans. The O-Hi-O, now she's a gentle river, it's true. But she turns into something else down Illinois way. The mother of them all, she is, raging and muddy. So right around the bendy parts of the Ohio, just before she swoops down south, there's a place called Cave-In-Rock. You can see it as you round the bend, and by that time, it's too late! You see, Cave-In-Rock is exactly that: a big old cave high up the bank in a limestone cliff. And there is people in that cave you wouldn't want to meet on any dark night, or any bright day, for that mater.

They that inhabits that cave was outlaws and the meanest, nastiest folk you'd ever come across. Oh, they are all chased out of there now I 'spect. That was back in the day before the Regulators got after them. Before my time, even. They wasn't the only ones, though. Let me tell it this way. I reckon the first gang of crooks that was in there was Sam Mason's. He used to be up at Diamond Island but I guess he heard about the cave being used by some counterfeiters and he knew the one of them, the Duff fellow.

Moved right in and started all sorts of mayhem. He ran a gambling den, with whiskey and women available for all sorts of unsavory characters. Then he got the idea to pillage the boats that came down the river.

They had different ways of doing it. Sometimes they'd just wave real friendly like and invite the boat people in to stay the night or have a few, I don't know. Then they looked through the boat and took away anything valuable. If anybody complained, well, they ended up in the river! Sometimes they'd get somebody to flag down the boat up river, you know, for a ride. They'd look around and if the people was poor and needy, they'd just let 'em go by. But if they had cash or gold or silver, why, they would signal to Mason and his gang and the boat would get stopped right there by the cave, the treasure looted and the boat sent on its way. No complainin' or it's into the river with ya!

Then the Harpe brothers come along. They was blood thirsty killers. They started out from Louisville and had three wives between the two of them, figure that out. They was horse thieves and their first murder was a fellow turned 'em in. What they did to hide the body was to slit the fellow open and fill him with stones, then drop him in the river. But he floated up anyway and the law got after them. After that they just started killing 'cause they enjoyed it, I guess. At one point the women got caught but was let go and they all got to Cave-In-Rock. No traveler was safe going by that place. They pushed people over the cliff to their deaths. One man was tied to the back of a horse and they both got throwed over! They were so brutal that the other pirates finally tried to force them to leave.

Mostly the Mason gang would do things like sneak onto the flatboats at night and bore holes to sink them. But they killed too. There was a guy named Colonel Plug. He came along after Mason and the Harpes left. The Regulators, they chased 'em all out. A Captain Young it was, from up at Mercer County, that formed them vigilantes to run down the outlaws. Killed one of the Harpe brothers, I believe. Chopped his head right off. And the Mays, the Wilsons, and their lot were fleeing for their lives.

Well, it was a pretty dangerous place. Even the so called authorities left it alone. Up river a ways was a place where people could cross the river on a ferry. Called Ford's Ferry and run by a James Ford who was a well known civic leader and socialite fellow with a secret life as an outlaw. He was tied in with the James Wilson gang and would direct the pirates toward the unsuspecting river travelers. He was eventually murdered, by who, nobody knows. And up the road from the Ford's Ferry was the Potts Inn, and it's there my story really begins.

We had all heard the story of Billy Potts. Billy was Isaiah and Polly Potts' son who'd gone away from home as a young man. The tavern they ran, you see, it was near Ford's Ferry and the cave and it had a reputation that travelers stopped there and were never heard of again. They say there were unmarked graves all around and the well ran red with the blood of their victims. Was it true? Who knows. But Billy, he was headed home after some years and grew a long bushy beard such that nobody recognized him. He was met at Ford's Ferry by one of the henchmen who determined that Billy was carrying a bag of money—a great deal of money. So the word went out that here was a rube ripe for the plucking.

Billy got to his parents' inn up on Potts' Hill and went to the well to get a drink. Isaiah, eager to acquire the money, dispatched him with a hatchet and threw him down into the well, not realizing it was his own son he had killed. Billy wasn't so innocent either, though, they say, as he had been in with some outlaws back in Kentucky. Isaiah drew the body back out of the well in order to bury it proper like, just as Polly come up and her seeing a birthmark on the youth's neck, screamed out, "That's our son Billy!"

So I'm telling all this to lay the groundwork for what was to come. You can see what that area was like, that the people were ruthless, greedy, despicable people. Now I'd been on barges and flatboats for some years and I'd been by the place many times, never seeing any strife nor been accosted by any outlaws. We figured it was mostly rumors, but I will say we tended not to tarry around Cave-In-Rock.

This day we were headed down river with the pigs and as we were getting close to Ford's Ferry we all began to tell those stories again. My mates were Big Pete O'Brien and Hartley Nichols and some others. Those two I won't ever forget. But the stories was flyin' back and forth, each teller intent on outdoing the next fella. It'd been ten, fifteen years since the Regulators come through and the worst of them was gone, or so we figured. But the tall tales lingered. The stories about Potts' Inn were particularly grisly, as they preyed on travelers from two roads that crossed there. Isaiah chopped them with an axe, Polly sliced them with a big butcher knife. Cut 'em up in little pieces right in the kitchen. Of course, we knew this was exaggerated, if there was any truth in it at all.

As we got to where the ferry was operated, Big Pete pointed out a woman up on the bank was waving her arms wildly and yelling at us. Well, we knew better than to stop, since this was a technique the river pirates used to lure their victims. But there was something about the woman, a real frantic kind of intensity that convinced you there was a need to investigate. Our Captain White didn't say no, so the tiller man steered us toward shore so's we could better hear what was being shouted. I tell you, it was awful just to hear the desperation in her voice. We could make out something like, "He's killing us," and "Bloody murder!"

As we swung close to the bank the woman jumped for the boat but was short and fell into the river. Big Pete pulled her up on board. She was sputtering and screaming and water dripped from her wet dress. There was a stringy river weed caught in her hair. She was the loveliest thing I'd ever seen and I fell in love with her instantly. She was able, between sobs, to blurt out that her sons were still up the hill and being in mortal danger. Captain White said for us three, Big Peter, Hartley and me, to go up there. We hurried up the slope to the inn on the hill.

We learned later that Bernice, that was her name, that she and her two growed sons, her husband being deceased, had been traveling by wagon along the Shaverstown Road on the way to Golconga. They'd got to Potts' Hill and seen the tavern there. They stopped to refresh themselves, the innkeeper being the most genial of hosts you could imagine. He put them so at ease they thought nothing of his suggestion that they sample the sweet water from his well out back of the inn. As they stood, passing the tin cup around, they were suddenly threatened by a man carrying a long handled axe. They tried to run to the wagon but found it had disappeared, I suppose taken by the highwaymen or the river pirates. "Run, Mother!" yelled her sons, and Bernice bolted down the hill towards the river, where she saw our flatboat approaching.

We hurried toward the hilltop. It was midsummer, but the ground was matted with dried leaves that crackled under your feet. It was densely wooded there, dank and dark, with the eerie feeling of a lonely, haunted place. Great black crows sat in the tree branches, seeming to laugh at us with their horrible cackling. The building loamed before us; it seemed balanced on the edge of the hill, as if the slightest breeze might topple its ugly bulk. It was two stories tall, with a porch and balcony running the width of the front side. You could easily imagine the ghosts of abused and battered souls leering at you from that rickety perch.

Muffled yelling came from around the back of the building. We saw there a large, brutish man, axe in hand, pulling at the door of a shed and could better hear the cries for help coming from within. We sprang upon him, wrestling him to the ground and pinning back the arm in which he held the axe. This I wrenched from him with no small effort, and flung into the woods. Hartley announced our presence to the trapped men in the shed, saying succor was arrived. Cautiously, they crept out and saw we had their assailant down on the ground.

This would have ended it, save that two more ruffians came from out of the woods. They wore dirty clothes and muddy boots and carried each a spade or shovel which they swung wildly as they came. These two we could easily have bested, even in spite of the shovels, which I suspected they had used in digging a fresh grave, but for the appearance next of a woman, hair in disarray, slobber running down her chin, an evil glare burning at us from her eyes, and a huge butcher knife in her hand. "Get off him you b———s," she said. "I'll slice you to ribbons."

Her manner was so horrid and her fury so alarming, we all of us ran. The two sons and the three of us reached the flatboat and yelled for them to push off at once. The outlaws failed to pursue us, I suppose fearing our superior numbers. I would have delighted in feeding them to the pigs, however. We took the woman and her sons with us as far as Cairo, where they left the flatboat. I wanted so much to have the acquaintance of this woman I said to Captain White I would also leave the boat at that port.

The rest of the story is of no consequence, and more lengthy than you could endure, I 'spect. I married that sweet gal, and had a happy life together, we did. She died in '32 of the consumption, 'twas a sadness. I never again took to boating on the river, but as you see, I'm never very far from its familiar waters. I'm telling you all this because I see you are an innocent, the likes of which could be hassled by those rogues upriver, be they still alive. To warn you to be wary of strangers on the river. But you're a smart lad, I can see. I can only wish you a safe journey and that you find your heart's desire.

CHAPTER 16
THE FALLS OF THE OHIO

Louisville, Kentucky, 11 June, 1846

"Thunk!" The bowie knife pierced the soft wooden planking of the flatboat within inches of James's bare left foot. "Not bad," said Mary Jane, grabbing the knife by the handle. She then took aim and threw, rather than dropped, the sharp implement at a spot near her own bare foot. "Better!" she exclaimed. The game of mumbley-pegs attracted the attention of Lancelot, who sniffed at the knife stuck in the flooring, then decided lying in the sun on the upper deck might be a more rewarding occupation. The flooring was exhibiting a rash of knife marks by the time the game was curtailed, Catherine having heard the loud thunking. Her reprimand was harsh, but appropriate, pointing out to the two children the danger of poking a hole in the flatboat and sinking it, as well as, of course, the danger of slicing off a toe or two.

A few days ago on a particularly foggy morning, there had been a collision between a flatboat and a steamboat. The steamboat's pilot house was high above the fog bank and since the pilot could see both shores, he had called for "full steam ahead." The flatboat was directly in front of him. Too late he saw the boxy shape and called for an "all stop." Too late he reversed engines. The momentum of the large boat carried it into the flatboat, splintering it, flinging cargo and crew into the Ohio. Only minor injuries occurred and the crew was rescued, but the accident would result in a lawsuit that would linger for many months to come.

Isaac had wisely kept to the shoreline that day, even stopping when the fog was the thickest. Other boatmen took their chances, sometimes blowing horns or banging on the boat so to be noticed by the larger steamboats. It was surprising that more accidents didn't happen. The greatest fear for the river traveler lay in explosions of the boilers on the great paddle wheelers. This happened more frequently than any other kind of accident, and fire could spread from boat to boat, especially in the close quarters of a port.

But today was clear, a deep blue sky manifesting a few puffy clouds, the sonorous calling of loons, and an unusual sparseness of river traffic, adding to the tranquil wayfaring. Will and Dick were on the side sweeps. Lancelot lay on the deck between them on his back, his feet sticking up in the air.

"That dog sure looks comfortable," said Will.

"He does know how to relax, that's for sure. This is a good day for it. This river seems relaxed as well."

"It is kind of slow. You know, you see sometimes people tie their flatboats together. Sometimes three, four—with families on them. It seems like they go faster that way."

"That and they have a community. They even have dances. There's always a fellow with a fiddle."

"Be really hard to steer, though. And I wouldn't want to get in the way of a paddle wheeler!"

"Be nice to go to a dance."

"You miss Sara Ann a lot, don't you, Dick?"

"Sometimes it's all I think about. You'll see someday when you have a girl."

"Where am I going to find a girl on this river?"

A river like smooth, grey-green glass lay ahead of them, calm, cool, carefree, the reflections of tall pines rippling easily in their own shadows. There was nothing to portend misfortune. Gradually, after rounding a bend, the trees gave way to a gently sloping shore. The shore began to show signs of marsh: tall cat tails and mounds of floating green algae, broken now and then by the splash of a frog bent on escaping the long bill of a river bird. The river slowed even more and the flatboat entered an eddy where it turned nearly around, captured by the slowly swirling current. They leaned hard on the sweeps to straighten her, then paddled to attain the main channel of the river.

Ahead, they saw a town high on a hill, and out near the end of a pier they saw a man waving his arms and shouting. They were still struggling to escape the current which seemed intent on pulling them into the reeds and cat tails. As they neared the pier they could distinguish the man's words:

"Howdy, folks. I'm Pete Buchanan, the best danged riverboat pilot that Jeffersonville has to offer. Would you be needen' my services? I know ever crag an' slurry of them chutes an' I works cheap, I do."

The stories of river pirates fresh in their minds, Isaac and his family were not eager to hire on a stranger. Isaac waved the man off and they returned to fighting the river.

"Aye, you be headin' for the canal then, I 'spect."

Canal? Thought Isaac. I don't want to ever see another canal again! He leaned against the rear sweep and called for Will and Dick to paddle. At last, they broke free and were drifting down the center of the river. It flowed more swiftly now, a circumstance that pleased them—for the time being. They could see ahead another great island that split the river into two parts. To the left was a large city and the familiar shapes of docked steamboats. To the right, a broader channel presented itself, devoid of boats large or small. The current carried them toward this rightmost channel, gaining speed. And so it was there they headed.

"Hey, said Will, "it sounds like rain."

"But it isn't raining," said Dick. They heard a low roar that slowly increased in volume until they could identify it as the rushing of water against rocks. "Oh, oh! Rapids!"

Philip, who had been sleeping in the cabin, suddenly burst through the door and climbed the ladder to the upper deck. To his horror, he saw the wisps and flashes of white and heard the clashing of the water against the jagged rocks. "It isn't rapids," he said. "It's the falls."

"Falls? How can there be...?"

"I've heard about this. It called the Falls of the Ohio. The river drops over 25 feet here! We need to take the other channel."

"We can't! The current is too strong! We're headed for the falls!"

"OK," said Philip. "we can get through it. There are places. Look, see where the white water is. Those are rocks sticking up. Head for that spot between them where the water looks smooth. It's a channel."

But saying it was easy; doing it seemed nearly impossible. Isaac shouted for Philip to take the rear sweep while he stood lookout on the upper deck. "And get everyone else inside," he yelled. Emma pulled Lancelot out from behind a barrel where he was hiding and whimpering. They headed for the cabin, all, except James, who insisted on staying on deck. "You need me to spot rocks," he said.

The roaring was now so loud they had to yell and resort to hand signals. Isaac thought he had found a break in the white water that might be a channel and gestured to the boys to angle the boat toward it. The danger now was that the boat was swinging and threatened to turn sideways in the current. They leaned hard on the sweeps and straightened her, but the work was exhausting.

"Now paddle with all your might!" Isaac shouted to Will and Dick. If the boat could move even just a little faster than the rapids—they might have a chance. They entered the smooth section of river between two enormous boulders where waves crashed and sent spray into the air creating a blanket of mist that fell back onto the flatboat. Water surged against the sides and lapped over the high rail, spilling onto the floor boards making walking on the deck treacherous. There was a crash as the flatboat hit something and its progress halted abruptly. It now hung precariously over the edge of the falls, half in the river where the current pushed at it relentlessly, and half in mid air, ten or twelve feet above the lower rapids. The time it hung there seemed an eternity to the steadfast sailors. All held their breaths. Then suddenly, the boat tipped forward and slid down into the foam below. Water broke over the bow and flooded the deck.

It rocked, it bobbed, it swung in the waves, but it remained upright and afloat. No one had been swept overboard but all were drenched to the skin and shaking. The flatboat began to swing and turn, as it had in the eddy. Quickly, they saw to the sweeps and worked to point the nose of the boat down river with the current. The relief they felt at having survived the falls was short lived as they now had over two miles of rapids to negotiate. The river would drop another 12 feet and the current would carry them at

14 miles per hour, faster than a steamboat!

Isaac leaped to right a barrel that had tipped over and was rolling back and forth, crashing into crates and boxes. He pulled open the cabin door. "Is everyone all right?" he asked.

"We're okay," answered Catherine, although Katy was sobbing. Emma cradled her sister in her arms and placed a hand on Lancelot's neck, stroking the wolf pup to comfort him.

"It's not over yet. Everyone grab on to something and try to stay calm. We've got rapids to get past."

Oh, they were in for it: The first section after that initial drop was called the Indian Chute. River pilots knew it well. Knew the Backbone Reef and Bone Rock, the Big and Little Eddies, and the islands—Corn Island, Goose Island, Rock Island and finally, Sand Island. If the water was particularly low, the limestone reef scraped the bottoms even of the flatboats.

In the early days, trade on the river was hindered by the Falls. Boats traveling with goods between Pittsburgh and New Orleans would need to stop at Louisville and portage their goods to another boat on the other side of the falls. Only in the highest level of water would the largest flatboats, Kentucky boats, and broadhorns attempt to cross over the falls, and then, only downriver.

As early as 1830 a canal had been built to route boats around the falls, and through the port of Louisville. It was built too narrow for the larger steamboats that traveled the river in the mid 1800s, but it would have sufficed for Isaac and his family. Had they taken the road most traveled, they might have avoided the strife of the rapids and whirlpools and sandbars and reefs of the chutes of the Falls of the Ohio. Had they been in the canal they might have heard an old fiddler on a flatboat singing this song:

Some rows up
But we floats down
Way down the Ohio
To Shawneetown

And it's hard on the beach oar

She moves too slow
Way down to ShawneeTown
On the Ohio

Now the current's got her
And we'll take up the slack
Float her down to Shawneetown
And we'll bushwhack her back

Whiskey's in the jug, boys
Wheat is in the sack
We'll trade them down in Shawneetown
And bring the rock salt back

I got a wife in Louisville
And one in New Orleans
And when I get to Shawneetown
Gonna see my Indian Queen

The water's might warm boys
The air is cold and dank
And the cursed fog it gets so thick
You cannot see the bank

Some rows up
But we floats down
Way down the Ohio
To Shawneetown

The water swirled and foamed and formed a great wave that pushed the boat along. More waves were surging over crags creating geysers of spray and the river gushed around great ledges of limestone forming cascades that grabbed at the flatboat, buffeted it, twisted it, pulled it perilously close to the rocks. Crates and barrels were jostled and slid around the deck. The men held on for dear life as they rode the fury of the river down the Indian Chute. They felt the bottom of the flatboat grinding against a limestone ledge where the river became shallow. Then the reef fell away and they plunged into the depths of a hole as sheets of water flew into the air, enveloping the flatboat. They grazed boulders and bounced against crags. They were sluiced through narrow chutes as helpless as a leaf in a deluge.

The river narrowed and snaked along Goose Island. They caught the edge of the Big Eddy, a raging whirlpool, and it flung them back into the main current. Here the Middle Chute, a shallower passage from the opposite side of Goose Island, merged and the river widened again. They passed two small islands and suddenly their wild ride ended. The river was as calm as if it had never kicked up such a fuss. The doldrums of the widened Ohio now seemed as shocking an anomaly as the tumultuous rapids had. Isaac quickly examined the flatboat for leaks or cracks but found none. "Of course not," said Will. "I told you this boat was ship shape."

CHAPTER 17
A DAY IN THE LIFE

Ohio River, near Alton, Indiana, 14 June, 1846

With the dawn came the cacophonous chorus of hundreds of frogs. Dragonflies darted among the rushes and the frogs' long tongues whipped out at them. A doe stood on the river bank transfixed by the alien shape of the flatboat. The solid darkness had gradually grayed, then seemed to glow from within in tints of brown and green. As the flatboat rocked in the wake of a passing steamboat the three sleepers on the deck, Dick, Will and James, stirred from their dreams and stretched. Lancelot jumped onto Will's stomach and licked his face. "Hey, pup! Good morning!" he said. The sky upriver dissolved through pink to orange, then lightened to a delicate cerulean. Bird song began to rival the frog symphony.

In the cabin, Isaac tumbled from his bunk to find that Catherine was already up and placing kindling into the cook stove. "Good morning, Cat," he said. And, "Thank you, Lord, for another day." As Catherine worked she sang a verse of an old Scottish folk song called "The Wraggle Taggled Gypsies," which her mother had taught her:

> What care I for a goose-feather bed?
> With the sheet turned down so bravely, O!
> For to-night I shall sleep in a cold open field,
> Along with the wraggle taggle gypsies, O!

Katy was up, out of bed and pulling the light blanket from Emma who complained, "Mother! Tell Katy to stop it!" But mother wasn't about to take Emma's side this morning. "Get up, you sleepy-head!" she called. Then one by one the sleepers awoke and ran for the latrine where a line formed hastily, the last in line having to be the one to empty the bucket. Lancelot jumped over the rail to perform his own constitutional on the river bank, then began chasing frogs. "Come, Lancelot! Food!" called Emma. That was all it took for the wolf pup to bound back onto the flatboat.

Hot coffee and oatmeal, a few of yesterday's hardened biscuits drenched with molasses, and the flatboat pushed off into the current. The sun rose, warm on their backs. The day had begun. "Dishes," yelled Catherine, and the girls dragged out the wooden wash bucket to fill with river water and soap powder. Bowls and spoons and tin cups splashed into the bucket and Elizabeth and Emma went to work scrubbing while Mary Jane and Katy unrolled a large towel on the deck floor. Lancelot tugged at the towel and had to be chased away before the drying could begin. The cast iron pot then sank into the wash bucket to the groans of the girls: their least favorite chore was washing pots and pans.

John and Philip took the side sweeps while Will sat in the prow as lookout. The river ran smooth and clear today, so Will figured he'd have little to do. Isaac sat at the tiller.

"Come children—lessons," Catherine called. "Emma, bring the slates. James, get the McGuffeys." There were more groans as Catherine organized her little floating schoolhouse. To Emma she gave McGuffey's Pictorial Eclectic Primer, with its pages of drawings representing letters of the alphabet. There was, for instance, Ax, Box, Cat, Dog and Elk and detailed drawings of each. The words were spelled in capitals and in lower case. "Start Katy on her letters, Emma. Then I want you to help her write them on her slate. While she's working on that, you can work on your cursive writing."

"Yes, Mother," answered the girl, taking Katy by the arm and sitting in the shade of the boat rail.

"Elizabeth, take the Second Reader and work on lesson one. I will want you to read it to me out loud. Mary Jane, take the Third Reader and work on lesson two. We'll answer the questions at the end of each chapter. And James?"

"Yes, Mother?"

"You may start on The Eclectic Fourth Reader. Read the first lesson."

"But Mother, I read it yesterday."

"You learn through repetition, James. Besides, there are some big words you didn't know yesterday. You will learn them today. Now, you children get started and I'm going back to talk to your father. When I return you can show me your progress."

Catherine climbed up on the roof of the latrine, where the rear sweep was mounted. Isaac smiled at her. "Come to visit me at work, my love?" he said.

"Yes, Isaac, I have."

"Is there something you want to tell me?"

"Yes, Isaac, there is." They drifted down river in slow harmony with breezes that whispered through the trees and sent willow branches swaying gracefully. A fish jumped, ripples expanding where it had reentered the water.

"Cat, I think I know. You are with child again, is that it?"

"Yes, Isaac. I'm sorry I didn't tell you sooner. But..."

"But you thought I'd delay the trip. And you are right. I would have done so. But Cat, are you...are you sure you'll be up to it? The traveling, I mean."

"I'm at five months. I'm surprised you didn't notice it."

"Perhaps I did. Perhaps I waited for you to tell me. And perhaps I am very happy we'll have another..."

"Son? Daughter? Oh, Isaac, do you want another son?"

"Cat, the Lord will give us what he knows is best. We'll love it and cherish it no matter if it's boy or girl."

"A son would help with the farm. Philip and John are grown. They may not stay so long as you would need."

"We'll see, love. We'll see."

The lessons were progressing as might have been expected with the teacher absent. Katy drew faces instead of letters, although Emma scolded her and did, in fact, produce a splendid example of the cursive alphabet. There had been some giggling between James and Mary Jane which was curtailed as their mother approached from the stern of the boat. "Let's start with Elizabeth," Catherine said. "Recite, please." She began:

Frank, what a fine thing it is to read. A little while ago, you know, you could only read little words, and you had to spell them — c-a-t, cat; d-o-g, dog. You were a long time getting through with the "First Reader," but now you can read quite well.

"That's very good Elizabeth. Now, Mary Jane, what is 'The Rule'?"

"Avoid the habit of clearing your throat by coughing, or making other unpleasant noises as you begin to read aloud."

"Very good. Now, tell me what the subject of this lesson was."

"Um, it was Rashness. One should always be careful to guard against rashness."

"Excellent. James?"

"Yes, Mother?"

"Read."

"OK, uh... You have often asked me to describe to you on paper an event in my life..."

"Go on."

"...which thirty years later, I can look..."

"Can NOT look."

"...cannot look back to without horror. No words can give me an ad... ad..."

"Adequate. Now I want you to work on that word. Emma? Let's see what you and Katy have been up to."

And so the lessons occupied most of the morning. Catherine was not unforgiving in her application of pedagogical discipline, but she constantly stressed the importance of learning, especially to be able to read fine books, books she hoped one day to acquire for her family. Shakespeare, Longfellow, even that Mr. Dickens. And the McGuffey Readers presented the children with a range of vocabulary, a set of ethical rules, and a respect for God and family, that would elevate them above the common, uneducated men and women of the day. Although her children could not attend regular school during the trip down the river, Catherine was unwilling to relinquish their study of language, history, mathematics and culture.

They'd been on canal and river now for three long

months. Their days were filled with routine: the men taking turns on the sweeps and the women seeing to the domestic chores. There was a time for work, for study and for play. Emma loved her dolls of sewn cloth stuffed with cotton batting. She shared an imaginary doll scenario with Katy. Elizabeth played Jacks and then jump rope. It happened that Dick was helping Catherine to reorganize the supplies in the barrels out on the deck. This meant that the cabin was not occupied. James nudged Mary Jane and whispered, "Mary Jane, come with me. I want to show you something!"

In the cabin, James pulled the foot locker from under his bunk and dug through wadded clothing, extracting a bundle: something heavy wrapped in an old shirt. He carefully unfolded the cloth, exposing the Colt Paterson Five Shot Revolver.

"James! What...where did you get..."

"I, uh, found it. Pretty neat, huh?"

"Father will skin you alive if he finds out, James. But... can I hold it?"

"Sure, go ahead. Just don't pull back the lever."

"It's loaded?"

"Well, of course it's loaded. What good is a gun that's not loaded?"

"But, James, what are you planning on doing with this," asked Mary Jane, taking the heavy revolver, peering across its sights, and swinging it around the room.

"Don't point that at me! Well, it's just in case, that's what."

"In case?"

"Here, quick, give it back." He rewrapped the revolver and stuffed it back in the bottom of the foot locker, just as Catherine entered the cabin.

"Go outside and get some air, children," she said. And they did.

On the upper deck, John and Philip had an easy time of it as the current flowed slowly and steadily. The river was deep here, and snags and sandbars were few and far between. They passed the time in conversation.

"I hope Jacob is well. I wonder if he got to Saint Louis. Say, Missouri is a slave state, isn't it?" said John.

"It is, but I heard there's abolitionists there. He'll find them, I'm sure."

"The Underground Railroad?"

"Yes. I just hope he steered clear of Shawneetown, that's all."

"Shawneetown? Where's that?"

"It's along the river in Illinois, we'll be passing it in a few days."

"But," said John, "isn't Illinois a free state?"

"That's another story that Bill Strunk told me. There's a lot of salt mines around there. People getting rich digging up the salt. Only they use slaves to do it. It's a special exception to the rule, just for the salt mines.

"Old Bill told me about this big old mansion up on a hill there. A man named Crenshaw owns it. It looks like a Greek temple, with pillars. Three stories tall. And the upper story, they say, is filled with cells where they keep the slaves at night. And Crenshaw, he's not above kidnapping free blacks and selling them into slavery. He's got a wooden leg. They say a slave took an axe to him one time and chopped off his leg!"

"Oh, next you're going to tell me that the place is haunted."

"Could be. It very well could be."

Afternoon evolved into evening. Dusk came as gradually as had the dawn. As the sun descended it cast a golden glow on the river before them. They nestled the flatboat against the shore, sending frogs and insects scattering. Traveling at night in the unwieldy flatboat was far too dangerous. Now it was a time for a leisurely meal, stories, catching fireflies and watching for shooting stars. Lancelot snuggled against Emma while Catherine read her and Katy a story from one of the McGuffey readers, a story about the King of Persia and a little dog. Was there a smile on Lancelot's face? If wolf pups could smile, Lancelot would, and did.

CHAPTER 18
CAVE-IN-ROCK

Ohio River near Cave-In-Rock, Illinois, 22 June, 1846

Not all the flatboats on the Ohio carried families. Most were laden with goods bound for New Orleans: cattle, pigs, corn, flour, whiskey, and other commodities. The larger Kentucky boats had on them as many as fifteen river-hardened men who propelled the boats with poles and oars or dragged them from the banks with long ropes when the river was shallow and the current slack or when sandbars stranded them. After offloading their cargo in New Orleans they would sell the boat for scrap lumber and return overland to Louisville, Cincinnati, or Pittsburgh, and start again with a new load. It was a rough life and they were rough men. An old minstrel song written by Dan Emmit in 1843 says it well:

> When de boatman blows his horn,
> Look out old man your hog is gone;
> He cotch my sheep, he cotch my shoat,
> Den put em in a bag an toat em to de boat.

> Den dance de boatmen dance,
> O dance de boatmen dance,
> O dance all night till broad daylight,
> an go home wid de gals in de morning.

> High row, do boatmen row,
> Floatin' down the river Ohio

There was such a boat moored at Diamond Island where the river seemed to split into two separate channels. Large and imposing, rife with sugarcane, timber and whitetail deer, Diamond Island had been the hideout of river pirates like Sam Mason and the Harpes. It had been the scene of the bloody massacre of an immigrant family by Indians as late as 1803. When Isaac and his family approached the large island two days ago, they were hailed by the boatmen on the Kentucky boat. Did they want to buy a pig or a cow? Did they need flour, whiskey, corn? "No, we're well stocked," had been Isaac's answer, not wishing to mingle with the ruffian element he perceived them to be. He had swung the rudder around to point the flatboat down the opposite side of the island. Passing the Diamond Island and emerging into the river proper, they saw a small skiff being paddled swiftly down river before them. Had they been prone to fantasies, they might have imagined this small boat piloted by scouts for the pirates, reporting a prize to be taken to their confederates down at Cave-In-Rock.

But Isaac never looked on the dark side, never assumed the worst of people that he did not know, never instilled fear, prejudice or mistrust in his children. If he imagined anything, it was that the day would provide splendor and enchantment, born of the natural beauty of the river. Philip, however, his head full of tales tall and improbable, could imagine almost anything dire or dastardly. Like Isaac, he had no fear of the unknown, it was just that the evil deeds of mankind did not surprise him.

Another day and a half would put them at Shawneetown. Philip would feel the pain of the poor black men and women penned like animals in tiny repressive cells, shackled, starved, beaten. He would envision the slaves led down steep stairways to the underground tunnel, marched through it to the salt mines where they labored long days with little food or water. He would imagine the terror of the runaways being tracked down by Crenshaw's night riders. The abject horror felt by free blacks taken at night from their homes to be transported across the river into Kentucky and sold into slavery. Jacob's stories of plantation life in Virginia paled at the plight of those doomed to the salt mines in Southern Illinois.

Now they were two and half days away from Diamond Island, nearing Cave-In-Rock. It would be James who would imagine exploring the interior of that fifty-foot wide opening into shear stone, that den of iniquities and abominations, that lair of lawless and ruthless robbers and murderers of not so long ago. He would see himself, torch held high, examining hateful inscriptions on the walls, discovering hidden treasure troves of purloined silver plate and jewelry. He would hear the echoes of ghostly laments, the long gone shudders of the condemned travelers whose bodies, slit open and filled with stones, would sink into the gloomy depths of the O-Hi-O, accompanied by the scuttled flatboats that had brought them to this jeopardous rendezvous,

"Can we stop and explore the cave, Pop?" asked James. "The pirates are all gone, Philip said so."

"No, James, we can't. It is still dangerous, and anyway, we don't have the time to do so."

"Aw, Pop!"

"Enough!" Isaac straightened his hat and ran his fingers through his beard, secretly admiring the adventurous spirit his son had shown, albeit, in James' usual haphazard and often fatuous manner. Isaac didn't fear pirates, living or dead, but he wasn't convinced James would not break a leg in the cave or plunge over the top of the cliff. Or lead his sisters into peril of some kind. No, they would not stop.

Gusts wafted the boat from upriver, adding velocity to their progress as they rounded a bend and left the cave behind. They attended the sweeps, seeking to skirt the submerged roots and branches of fallen trees near shore. Dead limbs protruded from the shallows offering perches for herons and shielding the river bank from view. One great heap of tree trunks, half in and half out of the water, concealed a small boat containing two gruff and grizzled ruffians, who promptly paddled out into the wake of the flatboat.

"It seems strange," said John, pulling hard on the right sweep to turn the boat away from shore, "that those fellows tried to sell us a pig. Wouldn't they be taking their livestock down south?"

"Mighty strange," agreed Dick. "Makes you think."

Philip worked the rear sweep, the rudder of the boat, giving Isaac a well-deserved break. Elizabeth found her father leaning against the rail, his eyes partly closed. She wrapped her arms around his leg in an embrace which at first startled him, then brought a wide smile to his lips. He lifted her face with one large and calloused hand. "A fine day, little one?" he said.

"Father," asked Elizabeth, "why do they treat the black folks so mean?"

"Why, indeed. You see, Elizabeth, there are people, perhaps not really evil people, but people that have to feel superior to someone else in order to feel good about themselves."

"I don't understand, Papa."

"If they can lord over someone it makes them feel big, even though in reality, it makes them small... very small indeed. Plus, they are very greedy people. You see, the slaves do all their work for them."

"They must be very sad, then."

"You mean the colored folk?"

"No, the mean ones. They don't work to enjoy life and they hate other people."

"They hate them because they hate themselves."

"Oh, I see now, Papa. It's like they are upside down to the rest of us. Being bad makes them think they are good."

"That's it, little one. Someday that will all change. Someday."

There was a thump as the small skiff collided with the flatboat. Two men leaped over the side rail, one holding the skiff's bowline, the other carrying a very long musket. Only Elizabeth and Isaac happened to be on the lower deck, Dick, John and Will being forward and Philip at the stern. The man with the musket pointed it at Isaac and pulled the lock into a fully cocked position.

"Hey old man," he yelled, "get everybody out here. We're gonna swap boats, you an' us." The other man carried what appeared to be the bayonet from the musket. Lancelot came from behind a barrel and began to snarl menacingly. As Philip came bounding over the roof of the latrine, the man raised the bayonet. Philip stopped just short of its point and raised his hands. "I ain't kiddin'," said the musket man. "I'll shoot the girl first!"

"Philip," called Isaac, "bring everyone one out of the

cabin. Slowly, please. Don't frighten them." Philip complied and soon everyone was on deck, looking down the barrel of a well oiled musket, primed, cocked and ready to fire. Everyone, that is, except one. James had remained in the cabin, not from cowardice, but to retrieve a certain item he had secretly hidden away. In case.

"That everybody?" questioned the musket man. "Go see," he said to his companion in menace, and the bayonet man walked quickly to the cabin door and threw it open. There stood James, the Colt Patterson Five Shot Revolver pointed at the man's stomach. The man uttered a curse so vile that Isaac covered Elizabeth's ears, then the man bounded across the deck, nearly knocking down the musket man, and leaped over the side.

The musket man, undaunted by this new turn of events, swung his weapon toward James but it was his misfortune to have needed the split second necessary to aim down the long barrel and so, by the time he had raised the musket to his shoulder and sighted on James, all he saw was a burst of flame and a puff of smoke as James had already pulled the trigger. Splinters of wood flew as the bullet bored a hole in the rail next to the man's leg.

"Place the musket on the deck and get off this boat. I have four more shots and the next one I'll put into your gullet!" said James, trying to conceal the shaking of his legs and the sweat rolling down his forehead. Now the man, seeing the wisdom of a hasty retreat, dropped his weapon and jumped over the side where he thought the skiff waited for him. There was a loud splash, more angry words that made Isaac cringe, then the flailing and flapping of arms and legs as the man attempted to swim ashore.

"Too bad there are no sharks in the Ohio," said Philip. Then: "James! James, you've saved our skins, you wonderful moron. Where did you get that revolver?"

"Yes, James," said Isaac sternly, "where did you get it?"

"It was a present from old Ephraim Vail, at the general store. When he heard we were leaving. He gave it to me for protection," James lied. Isaac was about to protest the irrationality of this explanation, but Catherine touched his arm with that special, gentle, touch that all men know instinctively means, "Shut up!" And so, all he said was,

"Give it to me. Any shells you have too. I will keep it now. Just in case."

"Well, anyway," said John, examining the weapon the would-be pirate had left behind, "now at least you've got a rifled musket."

The excitement over, the journey continued without further turmoil. They drifted six more days, past Elizabethtown, past Golconda, where in 1838, the Cherokee Nation, forcibly marched from their homelands to relocation in "Indian Territory," (as Oklahoma was then called), along the "Trail of Tears," spent a cruel, icy cold December. To keep them warm, the Cherokees were given used blankets from a hospital in Tennessee where there had been a smallpox epidemic. They had to wait in Golconda for the ferry, where the ferryman gave preference to anyone and everyone who was not a Native American. The ferryman charged them one dollar each, instead of the usual 12 cents. Many died of the severe cold and exposure. And Southern Illinois gained a yet another host of ghosts.

By June 28th, they had reached Cairo, Illinois, at the confluence of two mighty rivers, the Ohio and the Mississippi. Positioned on a long finger of land formed by the winding Mississippi, Cairo was thought to be protected by its levees from the threats of floods from the two great waterways, but the floods of 1840 and 1844 had shown its residents the dangers of overconfidence. Yet this strategically located town prospered by providing wood for steamboats traveling up and down the rivers. Isaac and his family would leave the gentle Ohio here and proceed up the tempestuous Mississippi. Their journey would now take on quite a different character.

CHAPTER 19
THE FLOATING PALACE

Cairo, Illinois, 28 June, 1846

"Sure, we'll tow you up the Big River," the man shouted down to Isaac from the Texas deck of the steamboat. "That way if we run out of wood we can chop your boat up to feed the boilers!"

"Thanks, but we'll look for someone else," answered Isaac, discouraged after spending all day going from steamboat to steamboat along the wharf in Cairo, looking for someone willing to tow their flatboat on the Mississippi.

The southern part of the state of Illinois was known as "Little Egypt," some said because, cradled between the Ohio and Mississippi river valleys, it resembled the Nile delta in Egypt, although few from Illinois would have visited that part of the world to compare it. Others said it was because severe droughts in the early 1800s had forced northerners to travel to the region to obtain grain, the way Jacob's sons, in the Bible, had escaped famine by migrating to Egypt. Or was it the naming of towns after Egyptian and Middle Eastern places that gave the region its moniker? Besides Cairo, there were the towns of Thebes, Sparta, Karnak, Palestine, Lebanon, and New Athens. To the south there were Memphis, Tennessee, and Athens, Georgia. But the nickname, "Little Egypt," predated many of these towns.

Most immigrant settlers in Little Egypt actually hailed from Germany, Scotland and Ireland. Perhaps the fascination with all things Egyptian stemmed from Napoleon Bonaparte's conquest and subsequent archeological looting of Egypt in 1799. Whatever the reason, poor little Cairo would never attain the grandeur of its namesake. The soil on which the town was built was sandy and water crept up into the city streets. The river flooded periodically. Levees built to withstand the flooding often failed. The principle obstruction to the economic success of the city, however, was the self interest, the greed and corruption of city officials and the owners of the Cairo City and Canal Company whose ineptitude and constant bickering stifled Cairo's potential. The river pilots hated the city. Flatboat entrepreneurs were charged exorbitant fees to proffer their wares on the wharf. Only the connection to Northern Illinois via the Illinois Central Railroad insured at least momentary economic survival.

Isaac and Philip had docked in a swampy area just east of the sprawling levees and wharves on the Ohio side and searched for passage northward on the Mississippi, only possible for their flatboat if a steamboat would tow them against the swift current. So far, their search had been fruitless. As they trudged, crestfallen, back toward their boat, Philip thought he spied a familiar face exiting a waterfront saloon. He hurried to intercept the man.

"Thomas Hardy!" Philip called. The man turned and instantly recognized Philip.

"Philip, my boy! 'Tis good it is to see you!" Thomas Hardy had been Philip's comrade and confidant during his tenure as a deck hand on the steamboat, Messenger.

"Fortuitous, indeed! Thomas, this is my father, Isaac Grosh."

"Howdy and halloo. Any father of Philip's is a friend o' mine!"

"Thomas, we've got our flatboat moored here at Cairo and we are looking for a steamboat to tow us up the Mississippi. No one seems willing."

"Aye, the boys is not fond of flatboaters or rafters. Too many collisions. Too many broadhorns blockin' the chutes or travelin' at night with no beacon."

"But some get towed, certainly."

"I may be able to help you with that. I'm off the Messenger and on a fancy showboat now, but I knows a few of the lads here abouts. Let me ask around. When they knows you be a chap o' mine I darest say they'll be more agreeable."

"That would be really helpful, Thomas."

"Come tomorrow to the showboat. It's Spelling and Ross' Floating Palace, docked just up the levee a ways. Come see the show if you've a mind. I'll have something figured out for ya."

Evening on the riverfront at Cairo, Illinois, was not the spectacular event you might witness in Cincinnati or Louisville, with the lanterns of hundreds of steamboats sparkling across the water like a million fireflies. Yet a few dozens of paddle wheelers were lined up here helter skelter, and the dying embers of their open boiler fires cast rivulets of gold and amber across the darkened Ohio. Wisps of black smoke rising from still smoldering logs snuffed out stars and deepened the night. Here and there, there were lanterns that swung and blinked as the Ohio rolled under the keels of boats and barges. It was just past new moon and the waxing silver crescent seemed the only pure source of illumination not obscured by smoke.

The family said goodnight and curled up on their bunks to sleep or read by candlelight. Eventually, deep breathing punctuated by the occasional snore signaled to two of their number that now stealth and nimble haste were in order. And so two dark figures slipped over the side of the flatboat and dashed along the levee. The story told by Philip at supper had piqued the interest of James, and together with his usual partner in crime, Mary Jane, he was determined to find out what went on at a "Floating Palace."

The showboat was not hard to spot. Bright lights, tinkling bells, and a bustling crowd of people heralded an activity quite alien to the nighttime waterfront. A hawker called out offering tickets for the show at an extravagant twenty-five cents per seat. A banjo player strummed and a fiddler fiddled as dancers tapped tambourines from a balcony on the upper deck of the boat. Boat, it was not, however. It was, in fact, a good sized barge upon which had been built an elaborately decorated, two story box, not unlike a paddle wheeler in appearance, but without engine or paddles or great spark-belching smoke stacks or glass lined pilot house. The showboat was a floating theater which moved from town to town pulled by a tugboat. There was no room for boilers when seats for paying customers took precedent.

Along the side of the boat hung a banner which read: *"Spelling and Ross' Floating Palace, Featuring Major Cort and His Authentic Carolina Minstrels."* James and Mary Jane watched, intrigued, as throngs, or what passed for throngs in Cairo, Illinois, scrambled up the ramp to find seats in the auditorium.

"Where are we going to get twenty-five cents?" asked Mary Jane.

"You'll see," answered James, twinkles in his eyes. They squeezed into the line of patrons lumbering up the gangplank. When they were stopped by the ticket taker, James began to whine.

"Mommy and Daddy!" he cried. "They've left us here without our tickets!"

"What are you saying?" said the man.

"They went in already and we have to find them."

The ticket taker, suspicious of this ploy, was about to turn James and Mary Jane back, but a pudgy man wearing a top hat behind the pair in line began to berate the ticket taker.

"Let these waifs in, my man. And be quick about it!"

"But Sir, these children..."

"Do you know who I am, Sir? I am Mr. Gilbert C. Long, a trustee of the Cairo City and Canal Company. And I, Sir, can have your boat banned from the wharf! So let these kiddies go find their mother!"

And so, James and Mary Jane entered that wonder of wonders, the buoyant, bobbing amphitheater of music and drama, Spelling and Ross' Floating Palace. The interior appeared similar to what one might have seen in New York or Chicago, in a theater set for musical comedy, concert, or ballet. The seating consisted of chairs with caned bottoms arranged to give a view of the stage from every angle, unobstructed by pillars or columns. A balcony provided several "box seats" for the well-to-do who could afford the price. Gas lights lined the walls and provided footlights for the raised stage. The orchestra, or what passed for an orchestra, having no pit as was common in other theaters, were seated on stage. A red velvet curtain was drawn back on each side and secured with golden ropes. A painted backdrop depicted a scene of the deep South, with magnolias in bloom and tall trees hung with Spanish moss. Framed by the trees, a colonnaded, Greek revival style plantation house sat on a distant hill. James and Mary Jane found seats to the rear of the amphitheater. The orchestra, a string band consisting of two banjo players, two fiddle players, and a snare drummer, began to play.

Onto the stage marched the minstrel troupe, a dozen white men dressed in raggedy clothing whose faces were blackened with burnt cork. Exaggerated lips were drawn around their mouths in white grease paint, giving them a bizarre, comical, yet tragic countenance. They strutted and high-stepped, arm in arm until they were lined up across the stage. The leader yelled out, "De cake walk!" and the line moved again, prancing and swaying with a dance-like rhythm. The crowd applauded loudly. They were unaware of the irony of this exhibition: white men masquerading as black plantation slaves, doing a dance that satirized and mocked their white owners. The slaves had watched the pretentious whites doing the "grand march" at their balls and adapted a parody of their pompous gestures into their own folk dances.

"Those aren't really black men, are they?" asked Mary Jane.

"They're whites wearing makeup," replied James. "They look more like clowns, if you ask me."

"I don't understand. Why do they imitate black men like that?"

"Who knows? They think it's funny."

"Jacob Green doesn't look anything like those men."

The minstrels sat in a semicircle. At one end was a fat man with a castanet made from bones. He was called "Brother Bones." At the other end was a skinny man tapping on a tambourine. He was "Brother Tambo." The crowd all seemed to know the routine that followed, with a central figure, the master of ceremonies, named, "Mr. Interlocutor," announcing that "The overture will presently commence!" Songs and dances of the minstrel show, often used by pro-slavery whites to denigrate blacks, showing them as inferior beings who needed the "civilizing influences" of plantation life, were ironically based on the

African dances and style of entertainment the slaves used to cope with their misfortune, often in secret defiance of their owners.

Mark Twain later said that he admired the minstrel songs so much that he would have "little use for opera," if only the minstrel shows would come back. The famous abolitionist, Frederick Douglass, took another view. He said that the blackface performers were "the filthy scum of white society, who have stolen from us a complexion denied them by nature, in which to make money, and pander to the corrupt taste of their white fellow citizens."

After a brief song, Mr. Interlocutor began a comedy routine saying, "Say, dat's a nice song dey singin'. Do you like it, Brother Bones?"

"Shore, old hoss." answered Brother Bones, scratching his head. "Did you not know I's de one what writ it?"

"No Brother Bones. You tryin' ta tell me was you what writ dat preddy song?"

"Yes it was. I was possin' it for dat yeller gal I met down when I's at Bluff-her-low."

"Yes, at Buffalo. So what kind of a gal was she?"

"She was highly polished, you see. Her fadder was a varnish-maker."

"Whatsa madder wit you, Brother Bones. You all the time lying ta me."

"Ya, you know why dey don't put no lion on de wedder vane?"

"No...lying, not lion. No, why don't they put no lion up on de wedder vane?"

"It's too hard to get the eggs, you see."

The audience laughed and slapped their hands against their thighs. James and Mary Jane just looked at each other, embarrassed by the portrayal of the slow-witted Brother Bones. They nodded, a gesture that meant, "We've had enough." As they rose from their seats and turned to exit the theater, the string band struck up a melody and Brother Tamboo stood and began to sing:

> Come, listen, all you girls and boys
> I'm just from Tuckahoe;
> I'm going to sing a little song

My name's Jim Crow.

Wheel about, and turn about, and do just so;
Every time I wheel about, I jump Jim Crow.

I went down to the river
I didn't mean to stay
But there I saw so many girls
I couldn't get away.

Wheel about, and turn about, and do just so;
Every time I wheel about, I jump Jim Crow.

Out on the levee, Mary Jane said, "Well, I guess now we know what a 'Floating Palace' is."
"Yes," said James. "A ship of fools!"

CHAPTER 20
THE UNDERGROUND RAILWAY

Cairo, Illinois, 29 June, 1846

"Well met, young Philip," said Thomas Hardy. "And good it is to be flappin' me gums again with somebody with a zest for life! These lowlifes here on this showboat are dead from the neck up, I do believe."

Philip laughed. "Yes, it's good to see you too. And a surprise. I thought you'd be down in New Orleans by now."

"Well, that's a another story. But you're here to see if I found you a ride up the big river."

"And have you?"

"Indeed I have. I will take you to meet an old pal of mine, a captain of a tugboat that goes up and down 'tween here and Savanna. He'll tow you along with a barge or two he takes. We'll go as soon as my mate comes to relieve me of my watch."

They stood on the deck of Spelling and Ross' Floating Palace, watching the river traffic chugging along the Ohio. Great billows of black smoke issued from the tall smoke stacks as stokers threw pine tar on the fire to signal their departure. The morning was crisp with a slight nip in the air. Ducks floated in formation along the rotting posts of the wharf, scavenging for food scrapes thrown overboard from the boats.

"What can you tell me of Jacob Green," Philip asked Thomas. "I was worried when he spoke of St. Louis."

"Aye. That's a dangerous place for a black man. One of the worst. But that's a tale to tell, for we did sail up river and we did dock at St. Louis. And Jacob, he was set to jump ship there. I have to tell you, I'd grown fond of the man. What a spirit he has! He was convinced, you see, that his wife and child had made it to Canada a year ago."

"I didn't know he had a wife and a child."

"Oh yes, he did. They were sold away from the plantation. But he heard, as these slaves have a network, you know, that they escaped. They all head for Canada, ever since old England freed all their slaves, there and around their empire."

"But why St. Louis? Why didn't he just get off along the Illinois side of the river. Illinois is a free state. Missouri is not."

"Well, that's complicated. It's true, St. Louis is a hot bed of slave trading. Why, they have a slave market every morning right on the steps of city hall! Any black man found walkin' around without a pass is instantly thrown into the clink and taken to the slave market. Free or not! And the punishments they inflict for the most minor infractions would appall you. Whippings. Sometimes even a lynching. No, it's no place for a black man to go."

"Then why...?"

"There's kind of like two Illinois. The south, the part they call 'Little Egypt,' that's equally dangerous. You get caught there and you'll find yourself back in Virginia or Kentucky in a flash. No, he couldn't leave the Messenger for Little Egypt. Anyway, the Underground Railroad has certain places you have to go if you don't want to get caught.

"When we docked at St. Louis, I just knew I'd have to take Jacob under my wing or he'd end up on the auction block. And I'd been in St. Looey many times before. I knowed where this safe house was, that was part of the Underground Railroad. You see, I just had to go with him. To protect him, like.

"We waited for night, then we both packed up a kit bag with the barest minimum of clothes and a little food so's we could travel light, and slipped down the gangway onto the levee. It wasn't real dark, there being a big bright moon and all the lights from the steamboats and all, so we had to keep to the shadows. I needed to get my bearings so's to know which direction to sneak in. Saw a big church steeple up the hill and figured right where we were and which direction was the safe house.

"There was a guy named Lemp had a brewery called the

Western Brewery. There was a whole lot of old caves under St. Louis that the Injuns used to live in. The Cherokees, it was. Lemp used the caves to ferment beer in big wooden barrels. He had a house that connected to the cave system through a tunnel. He was the son of a German immigrant and an abolitionist. Runaways could go through the tunnel from the Lemp house and make it to a cave that came out right along the river. A boat could take them across the Mississippi to Alton in Illinois, where there are a number of safe houses. From there they could go up to Quincy and eventually to Chicago. It's still illegal to bring escaped slaves into Illinois. So they have to travel at night, from house to house. Anyway, that was the plan.

"It was the Lemp house we were headed for that night. It is a small one story brick house on the southwest side. We were only a mile or so from it, but we feared the patrols that roamed the city watching for runaways. We skirted the warehouse district near the river without incident and came to a neighborhood consisting of two story tenement buildings. Here there were still people out and about, the evening being unusually warm. Piano music came through an open window. Dogs barked. We clung to the shadows and moved as swiftly as possible without arousing the attention of the night dwellers.

"I was pretty sure the Lemp house was only a few blocks away and I began to relax my vigil. A mistake! For as we stepped out beneath a gas street light, I heard a shout. 'There goes a n——!' came a cry. And all at once we found ourselves being chased up the avenue by a gang of five or six young men, one or two of whom carried sticks or pipes which they swung wildly about in the air.

"I can tell you my heart leaped into my throat and I all but choked on my fear. We ran for it, ducking into alleyways and bounding over fences. I think a few dogs may have joined the chase for the barking grew louder. Worse still, was that I had more or less lost my direction. I knew not where we were or where our goal might be. But we saw a lonely privy behind a house and made for it, cramming our sweating, tired bodies into the little outhouse and pulling the door shut just as our pursuers ran past the yard. The dogs must not have smelled us due to the aroma of defecation surrounding our hiding place, for they led the gang away, barking enough to wake the dead. I've never been so grateful for such a stench as we had to endure that night! After a while, we cautiously crept out of the privy and tried to find our way to the Lemp house.

"Now, I have an excellent sense of direction on the river. I can tell if a horseshoe bend is north, south, east, or west, or zig-zagged and criss-crossed. But these cities! All squares and straight lines. Go round a corner and yer facing the opposite way. So I had to get up high somewheres to spot that church steeple. Wherefore I climbed up a drain pipe and onto a low roof and did spot it. But whereas I thought we'd been goin' sou'west, we were indeed a ways nor'easterly. We needed to backtrack but that meant the gang of thugs was between us and the Lemp house! Well, this was my plan: I'd steer hard to larboard and not trim out until I circled around to the other side of the house. Then nor'east would take us directly to safety. At least I hoped it would.

"I executed this plan and, as luck would have it, we saw the little red brick bungalow up ahead near the end of a darkened street. Off we ran and just in time, for we pounded on the door, were received into the house by the sudden jerk of arms, after which the door slammed and we heard, 'Hurry! This way!' There came pounding again on the door, and rude remarks I won't repeat.

"We found ourselves stuffed unceremoniously down a trap door into absolute blackness. Our breath came hard and fast and we tried in vain to quiet ourselves, our hearts pounding so loud I was sure we'd be discovered. Up above us were muffled voices, the rising pitch and wavering tone signifying to an angry exchange between our stalkers and our saviors. The banging of heavy boots shook the floor above us as the slave hunters searched the house.

"After a time it became quiet and the trap door was flung open. We were chastised for leading the ruffians to this lair. Luckily, they hadn't been 'official' slave hunters, only some local boys intent on reward money. We would have, said our hosts, been severely beaten had we been captured. Although I am a white man, by aiding an escaping slave, I would have been subject to imprisonment and possibly worse. Jacob would have been whipped and auctioned to the highest bidder. We were to reenter the tunnel and hide there until morning, in case the bounty hunters returned. Then, we would be given directions on how to navigate the labyrinth of tunnels and caves below.

"This time we were given a torch which burned brightly and allowed us to see the vaulted ceilings and brickwork arches of the tunnel. We were told to venture about a thousand feet into the tunnel, and there we would find somewhat more comfortable lodgings for what remained of the night. Thus we followed the tunnel, being careful not to turn at any of its branches, and presently we came to large chamber where we were astonished to find, among a forest of kegs and barrels, velvet lined couches and tables on which sat oil lamps. We lit two of these, extinguished our torch, and settled down, each on a settee, to await the morn.

"'Wake up,' said a voice the next morning. 'There's time enough to sleep in the grave!' And this, we acknowledged, was very, very true. Our rescuer showed us a crudely drawn map. 'This shows where the tunnel meets the cave and how to follow that to the river. You'll wait there until a ferryman comes to take you across. Now study this well, for I can't let you take it, least you be caught and our escape route revealed.'

"Now, I've memorized over 1,200 miles of the wiggliest, most island-speckled, ornery river in this known world. So a little curvy cavern didn't phase me none. But what gave me pause was a few of the names marked on this wrinkled and stained piece of paper. There was something called 'the bone area,' which I took to mean an old Indian graveyard. A second cave crossed just beyond this and several sets of stairs were indicated, meaning the level changed either up or down, I couldn't tell which. We could proceed on a straight course here, and indeed, the cave was wider, but our host suggested that dangers lurked ahead, one of which was a deep well, difficult to see in the murkiness of the cave. The longer route, a tunnel off to the right, came to a bend where a wooden bridge spanned an underground river. Caution was to be exercised at this point as the bridge threatened to collapse in the near future. At the next fork we were to stay to the left, or we would find ourselves trapped in an ever narrowing cul-de-sac.

"I wasn't heartened by the indication of an area called 'the narrows' which lead to one called 'the dragon's lair,' nor did I like the note which said to watch for deep water on the floor as the cave descended, then rose again to a level grade, but with a low ceiling where one was forced to stoop. Near the end of this section, we would encounter the 'pit of death,' a plunging drop off which was to be skirted along a slim ledge. There were several miles of this sort of thing, but the reward was a cave opening, high on a bluff over the big river. One could scramble down a treacherous path to an embankment, hidden from view from the river, by a stand of thick brush.

"Well, I've described the map, so you know what lay ahead of us. We had the torch, our kit bags and a grave determination to survive bats, the ghosts of Indians, bounty hunters, dragons, and anything else providence might throw at us. I knew that by now, the Messenger had left port, so I was committed, even if I didn't want to be. We had to see it through, and so we followed the Lemp tunnel to a hidden doorway, and thus entered the Cherokee Caves.

"You must understand that I am a man of the outdoors. Standing on the deck of a steamboat, the wind whistling past me, the glare of sunshine glistening on the water, room to wave your arms in delight at nature's wonders... these are the things that ignite my being, make my blood pump with the joy of being alive! So it is difficult even to relate what I felt in that gloomy, constricted hole of hell through which we stumbled, bumped, and tripped our way in an infinite darkness. Even in the widest passages I felt the walls and ceiling closing in on me. The air was so stale that the occasional rotten smell of something dead was a pleasurable reminder that we were still on earth, albeit, many hundreds of feet under it.

"As we came to each juncture or anomaly which we remembered from the map, we were encouraged. We weren't merely trapped in a nightmare, there'd be an end to it, eventually. Or, an end to us! At the wooden bridge I knew our journey was at least half over. The planks creaked and bowed under our weight and I suggested we go one at a time across the river as the sound of the rushing water beneath the bridge was not a welcomed one. Jacob Green showed genuine courage throughout the ordeal, more, I must say, than I could muster myself. He sprang across the ancient bridge and held high the torch for me to see my way.

"The pit of death gave us pause and I nearly turned back to take my chances with the slave patrols. We kicked some loose rocks into the pit and waited to hear them hit bottom. I do not lie when I tell you I think that pit was bottomless! A ledge about the width of a shoe ran around the edge of this abyss. The was no rope or railing to grip. With his characteristic bravado, Jacob started out along the ledge, shuffling one foot, then the other, hands seeking finger holds on the rocky wall. One slip and our venture would BE over for him, if not for me as well. When he reached the safety of the other side I breathed a sigh of relief, then realized it was my turn.

"Inch by inch I moved my feet along the narrow ledge. My body pressed against the damp, moldy cavern wall. A crack here and there, a hole or crag afforded me some support, but my knuckles were bruised and bloodied as I dragged them in search of each miniscule hand hold. I think I held my breath the whole way. Well, as you see, I made it across the pit of death without tumbling into its yawning gullet. I would brave the worst rapids and storms on the river before crawling through a cave ever again.

"At last we emerged at the cave's opening on the bluff over the Mississippi. Climbing down the crumbling sandstone was a joy compared to our passage through the Cherokee Cave. We sat on the sand along the shore and waited. A pirogue approached from the other shore and a single man rowed this to us. We climbed in, glad to be away from the horror of Missouri and on our way to Illinois. He left us on the opposite bank where another man motioned for us to climb onto a wagon. A tarp was pulled over us and we began the next leg of our journey, again in darkness. A few miles up the river bank we entered the small town of Alton, Illinois. I knew this to be an abolitionist town, though not without many aggressive pro-slavers. Here we were hidden in the Bethel Church then later transported, clandestinely, to the Everett house up in Quincy.

"There I parted company with that noble soul, Jacob Green, wishing him God's speed. He would travel from there to Chicago, Detroit, and then to Canada, where I hoped beyond hope he would be reunited with his wife and child. As a white man, of course, I could stroll levees of Quincy, Illinois without incident. And that is how I came to ship on the Floating Palace."

CHAPTER 21
A TUG CALLED ATTA BOY

Cairo, Illinois, 29 June, 1846

"You're a good man, Thomas Hardy," said Philip.

"Don't I know it. It isn't everyday I get to give up a good paying job on a major steamer so's I can waste away in a dismal swamp like this on a barge full of black-faced white men."

"You'll connect again with a big boat, I'm sure."

"I've actually a hankerin' to go to sea. Taste some salt for a change. Get up Baltimore way and sign on a steamer. Well, I see my relief is here, so we'd best be goin' to meet your ride up the Mississippi."

"Lead on!"

The tug boat was moored half a mile up the wharf, picturesque with her bright blue hull trimmed in red, her single black stack sporting three red rings and her glistening white deck house, which spanned two thirds of her length, trimmed in red and blue. Mounted on top of the deck house, just forward of amidships was a tall wheel house, rounded in front and squared off in the back, windows all around. She had two masts, unrigged. The foremast carried her bell, horn, and a lantern for a running light. The main mast had a crane boom for lowering her dingy. Her large rear paddle wheel seemed out of scale and gave her the appearance of a small, brightly painted toy boat, afloat in some child's bath water.

Indeed, the great steamboats dwarfed her, yet she was all of 100 feet in length and had a 24 foot beam. Her hull was Douglas fir and her 15 inch thick keel was lined with ironbark. She was more maneuverable than a big steamboat and could push or pull one against strong river currents with ease. Her main purpose was to pull barges loaded with coal, that black gold which had become a lucrative commodity in this day of the steam locomotive, the steel mill, and the steamboat. She would also take on a flatboat or two or a great lumber raft.

Across her bow, in large white letters was her name: "Atta Boy." Philip and Thomas paused at the gangway and Thomas called up to the ship. "Ahoy, Cap'n Grafton," shouted Thomas. "May we come aboard?" They were waved on by a slim, good looking man with a full, neatly trimmed white beard. He wore a dark coat with gold buttons and his cap, sitting squarely on his head, was decorated with gold anchor and wreath embroidery and a shiny gold band. His tie, although loosened, held together a starched high collar, and a gold watch chain dangled from his vest pocket.

"Captain Grafton, Sir. May I present Philip Grosh, the lad I spoke of to you yesterday?" asked Thomas.

"How do you do, son?" said Captain Grafton, pumping Philip's hand like he was a winch sweating a halyard. "I understand you are desirous of a tow up river, is that right?"

"Yes Sir, I have my family on a flatboat just to the east of you. We're headed up to the Rock River colony in Northern Illinois."

"I have one barge in tow and another flatboat with a family. You can hook on behind them. Have you the fare?"

"Depends. How much will it cost us?" Philip was concerned. His father, Isaac, had discussed money with him, as the eldest son and the person best suited to negotiate their travel. When he heard what the cost would be, his face fell and Captain Grafton didn't fail to notice. The captain shook his head and made clucking sounds with his tongue, about to lecture the boy on the perils and, especially, the expenses of river travel. Thomas, sensing the impending perplexity, offered a solution:

"My mate here, Philip, berthed on the Messenger as deck hand with me not so long ago. I'm thinkin' you might be availed of his services on your tug."

"Hmm...," thought the captain. "I have a second mate that's not returned for duty as yet. And I have to tell you, I'd not be unhappy if he didn't show. Well, young man, would you be willing to trade your labor for a tow?"

"That's ideal," answered Philip. "I learned quite a lot about steam boating during my time on the Messenger. I enjoy the work! Better than sitting around on an old flatboat, hoping you don't hit a snag."

"It's snags you'll be watchin' for and other duties. We're a small crew. Just, you, me, my first mate who'll take the night wheel, the engineer and the engineer's mate, and a couple of roustabouts. Have to be vigilant of the barges behind us and wary of the river dangers before us. If yer game, and Thomas here will vouch for ya, I'm thinking you best be bringing that flatboat up right soon as I want to slip out of here within the hour."

Isaac's flatboat was last in line behind another, which in turn trailed a long wooden barge heaped with coal. The little train of tug and barge and boats rounded the point of the peninsula where Cairo sat—a town struggling for survival against the odds of both economic insecurity and racial strife. They steamed into the muddy Mississippi and Philip began the second phase of his undesired profession as riverboat sailor, eager to please, willing to learn, and fascinated by the slim, immaculate, and precise Captain Absalom Grafton.

Catherine was busy organizing her onboard school, and the men found they had little to do save watching for the inevitable snags and sandbars. But as the Atta Boy's draft was greater than most paddle wheelers, she would lead them through the deepest channels where rocks or trees or sunken ships were as rare as hen's teeth. Will, by habit, climbed to the upper deck where the side sweeps had been removed from the oarlocks and tied down securely. He looked with curiosity across the bow toward the other flatboat, seeking a glimpse of its passengers. But the other flatboat, somewhat longer and wider than theirs, featured a tall deckhouse at the stern that blocked his view of its lower deck.

The first of many horseshoe bends in the great river brought them past islands so numerous, they were numbered instead of named. They passed inland waterways like Newcum's chute, where the Mississippi had started to cut across the promontory, trying to shorten its rush toward the Gulf. Other islands had names: Dogtooth, Buffalo, Goat, Goose, Cat, or simply, Big and Little. The river pilots knew them all and knew the reefs and shallows and snags that presented a hazard to navigation.

"I thought the Ohio twisted and turned, but this river!" exclaimed Philip to the captain as he stood next to him in the pilot house.

"She changes her shape every season, my boy. A good pilot needs to relearn her and watch for the signs."

"What are the signs?"

"See that smooth area with a kind of shadowy line along the front of it? That shows you there's a reef underneath it. The water slides along it smooth as a baby's bottom, but there's solid sand there can rip your own bottom right off if you cross over it."

"And those ripples by the shore? Are those rocks or snags?"

"No, that's just the water getting anxious as it approaches that chute up ahead by yonder island. Rocks can be well hidden. In low water, you see a slight ripple, but in high, the face is not tellin' much."

"The face?"

"The face of the river. She gives away her secrets to those who know her expressions. And she tricks those what don't know how to read her. For instance, there's an old wreck off larboard bow, about fifty feet off shore."

"You can see that? What does the river tell you that you can see that?"

"Well, actually, I know that's there 'cause I sawr her go down some years ago. She's deep, though. No worries this trip. If the water were low I'd skirt her proper."

"I'll bet there's a story to that."

"Indeed there is. Mayhaps I'll tell it to ya one of these days."

Will was on the upper deck of the flatboat, watching the dwindling sun. Lancelot stretched out beside him, nuzzling to be petted. The faint sound of a fiddle came from the flatboat ahead of them. They had just passed the small town of Commerce, Missouri, without stopping, a long day behind them, a long night ahead. As he scratched Lancelot's tummy, he heard a voice. Turning toward the other flatboat he saw a mop of red hair, then a freckled face peeking over the deckhouse.

"Hey! Hi, there! Whatja doin'?" came the voice. It belonged to a young girl, now head and shoulders rising above the deck as she mounted a ladder.

"Hello, yourself. Can you come closer? I can hardly hear you."

The girl was now on the upper deck, the roof, as it were, of the deckhouse. Will could see she wore a calico frock printed in a small, brightly colored pattern. Her feet were bare and her hair, instead of being pinned up, flew wildly in the wind.

"Why don't you come over here?" the girl said.

"Why, that's ten feet at least between boats! Are you crazy?"

"Maybe. What's your name?"

"Will, um... William. William Grosh. What's yours?"

"Cathy. Cathy Tennis. My real name is Catherine."

"Oh, that's nice. My mother's name is Catherine."

"How old are you?" asked Cathy. She stood with one hand on her hip, her weight on the opposite foot, giving her body a coquettish posture.

"I'm six...seventeen. How old are you?"

"I'm seventeen too."

"You are not! How old are you really?"

"I'm...fifteen."

"I'll bet you're more like twelve."

"I am not! I'm thirteen last September. I have four sisters and a baby brother. Daddy is from Pennsylvania and we're going to Illinois. What do you think of that?"

"I don't know. I have three brothers and four sisters. We're from Pennsylvania too and we're going to Illinois."

"I bet we get there first, 'cause our boat's in front of yours!"

Will was amused by the girl, and intrigued. She might become a interesting traveling companion for the days ahead. Yes, very interesting. Kind of young, rather annoying, but that gave her spirit. Yes, lots of spirit. Kind of cute, too. Will thought back to the day he had that conversation with Dick Cornelius about girls. Where would he ever find a girl on this river, he had asked. Maybe now he knew.

Catherine Tennis descended the ladder as the sun was now falling below the horizon. Her younger sister, Mary, came running up to her. Who were you talking to, she wanted to know. Oh just a boy. Was he cute. Yes, I think I'm going to marry him. Oh yes? Yes I am. Does he have a brother? He has three brothers. Well, maybe I'll marry one of them. The little sister taunted Catherine. Maybe you will and maybe you won't. Catherine stuck out her tongue at Mary. Yes I will. Mary reciprocated, her tongue waggling. The shadows grew deeper and they heard their mother calling them.

CHAPTER 22
TOWER ROCK — A GHOST STORY

Grand Tower Rock, Illinois, 30 June, 1846

Sailing the river at night was a novelty for the flatboaters. Philip had experienced it on the Ohio, and he was eager to spend some time in the pilot house as the tug, Atta Boy, crept up the starlit river. Neither darkness nor storm bothers a river pilot, Captain Grafton had told him. Nothing, except fog that hides the banks of the river and causes many a boat to sail into thick forests or crumbling bluffs. The first mate had been roused from sleep for his shift. Upon seeing Philip for the first time, he had exclaimed, "Who are you and where's my buddy?" The introductions had not gone well as apparently the man, Wilbur Bixby, was leery of this wet-behind-the-ears newcomer who had usurped his buddy's spot.

And a farther cry from Captain Grafton could not be had. First Mate Bixby was no where near as tidy. His coat was dirty and unbuttoned, his shirt tails hung out and his cap, if it could be recognized as such, was in a shambles and looked about to topple off his head at any minute. No full beard to mark him as riverboat pilot, he had only scruffy mutton chops, uneven and unruly. With a sneer he ordered Philip out of the wheelhouse. Philip went below, disappointed that he had not been able to befriend Wilbur Bixby.

In the morning Philip rolled out of his bunk and entered the wardroom where a steaming hot pot of coffee sat on a wooden table. In the galley the engineer had thrown several hunks of bacon on the grill and the aroma drifted into the wardroom, greatly enhancing Philip's outlook on the day.

There was no way to communicate between the tug and the flatboat of course, and Philip wondered how his family was doing.

The routine on the flatboat, in fact, was not much different than it had been on the Ohio, save that the necessity to beach for the night was eliminated. Catherine still held school for the younger children. Emma played with Lancelot, throwing a knotted piece of fabric which the wolf pup chased and shook menacingly, as if he were hazarding a small animal. Will spent much of the day on the upper deck, watching for the reappearance of a certain red-headed girl. John and Dick helped clean the deck and reorganize the boxes and barrels. Catherine and Isaac were finally able to spend some well-deserved time together.

"It won't be long now, my love," said Isaac. "Once we reach Savanna we'll look for an old friend who has been helping the Brethren find land. You remember Sam Funk, don't you?"

"I do. His father was named Samuel also, wasn't he?"

"Yes. He and Barbara were among the first to go west. Sam knows the lay of the land."

"A nice man. Do you think we'll find good farm land?"

"Illinois is young and fertile, and flat! So much easier to plow and plant than the hills back in Pennsylvania. I only wish I could have convinced Father to come with us."

"He's not so young as you, Isaac. And he moved once already. That's where you get your wanderlust, I think. From your father."

"Yes. Like father, like son, they say."

Philip was called to the pilot house by Captain Grafton early that morning. Did he want to take the wheel and try his skill at piloting? He grasped the big wheel with enthusiasm and at once discovered that skill at piloting also meant strength at keeping the tug straight ahead when the river pushed against the rudder and threatened to spin the wheel out of his hands. It was a thrill to stand up high above the river in the glass enclosed pilot house and swing the big boat and its train of barge and flatboats around the bends and past plantations and islands and the few reefs he now could recognize.

Up ahead Philip spied a towering island, nearly 90 feet high, topped with vegetation. The river swirled furiously along it. Captain Grafton, who had stayed close to supervise Philip's first attempt at river navigation, smiled, and waited to see what Philip might do as they approached the rocky tower.

"Captain! Look at that huge rock protruding from the river up ahead. It's like a small mountain."

"Aye, lad, ease on over to the other side of the river. But watch the shallows now. Just stay well off the tower."

"What is it, Sir?"

"That's the Tower Rock, son. The Frenchies called it 'Le Cap de Crocks'. Had 'em a big wooden cross up there many years ago. Them explorers, Markay, and Jolly-et found it."

"It looks innocent enough."

"The Indians told them there was demons lived there. I guess because of the roar of the river as she hits the back of that little cove there and comes rushin' back out. See that line of boulders, 'bout half a mile long? That's called the 'Devil's Backbone'. It funnels the river into a channel and forms a whirlpool that's sucked in many a keelboat in the day. That big rock is called the 'Devil's Bake Oven.' Even a big steamboat or two has smacked up again' that. Then, of course, there's the ghosts."

"Ghosts?"

"You see, in low water, you can hike over to the tower from shore. So many people are fascinated by it, they just gotta risk getting stranded there when the water rises. Fools they all are! Others take their boats too close and end up drowned."

"And they're the ghosts?"

"Naugh, not them. Anyway, the story goes, this nice young couple wanted to get married up on the tower. Well they did so and as they were leaving they got caught in the whirlpool. Their little boat was whipped around and dashed against the rocks. The were all killed except one fellow, a slave they had with them."

"That's terrible!"

"It was predicable. Well, a girl child was born that very same day to the bridegroom's sister back in town. Years later, there was a birthday party held for the girl up on the

Tower Rock—don't ask me why—their fascination with the place went beyond the tragedy, and beyond common sense! So is seems the slave was invited along to the party, I guess as a sort of remembrance for the dead from the wedding. As they all looked out over the big river that day there was a mist come up and it thickened. It formed into solid shapes that looked like men and women. It seemed to them that the wedding party what had been swallowed up previous was rising up from the depths!"

"The ghosts!"

"Indeed. The wedding party sort of wafted over to them in the breeze and the priest handed the slave a rolled up parchment, still dripping wet from the Mississippi. They faded back into the river and were never seen again. When the parchment was examined, it was found to be a prophesy. It said that a great war was to come, that families would fight one another and sadness and grief would rule the land."

"But no war came."

"Not yet is hasn't. It's a good story, though. It shows you how a place like that, where so many people has met their deaths through accident or foolishness, can be a focus for warnings from the other side of the vale. I'd be wary of the place even if it weren't a danger to my ship."

"A great war, huh? You know, we Brethren don't cotton to war. We don't believe in fighting and killing one another. We don't like slavery, though. If there was a war come to settle that issue..."

"Would you fight in that, young Philip?"

"I'd not carry a gun in a war. But I'd fight in other ways. We'd help the slaves get their freedom. You can be sure of that."

"That's honorable. Well, I hope it never comes to war. Now keep to the center of the river, lad. We're making good time. Don't need no ghosts chasing us today!"

As the tug passed up river from the rock Philip glanced back toward the huge edifice. It seemed to him that a thin mist rose from the river, swirled and danced, then slowly faded.

"Hey you, help me up!" Will was startled by a voice that

seemed to come from below the bow of the flatboat. He had sat on the upper deck that morning and looked at the looming Tower Rock as they floated by it. The girl, Catherine Tennis, had shimmied hand over hand along the tow rope that stretched between their boats, dangling above the river with her feet inches above the waves. "Come on! Give me a hand!" she cried.

"For the love of...what are you doing down there, you little fool?"

"I'm dancing a jig. What do you think I'm doing. I'm about to go for a swim if you don't give me a hand."

Will grasped the girl by the wrists and pulled her to safety. "That's the stupidest thing I ever saw. Don't you know those boats could collide together while you're hanging there in between them? Golly!"

"Is that all you can say to a girl that's braved the terrors of the deep to come see you? Golly? Better I should climb back home."

"No, wait! It's really not safe. Come down to the lower deck. Meet my family, but tell them you flew over to see us. They'll not be happy to hear I let you climb on that rope."

"You didn't *let* me do anything, you dodo. I do what I want."

"That's what I'm afraid of."

They climbed down the ladder to the lower deck. Cathy stopped short. "Eek!" she cried. "There's a wolf down here!"

"That's just our dog, Lancelot. He won't hurt you."

"Dog my left elbow. I know a wolf when I see one."

"He's a dog, I tell you. And he's just a pup, anyway."

"A wolf pup, huh? Wait 'til his mommy comes lookin' for him."

"Won't happen. He's an orphan."

"An orphan wolf pup, hitching a ride up the Mississippi on a flatboat with a knuckle headed..."

"Please don't call him a wolf, Cathy. People might think ill of him. Is it that red hair that makes you so ornery? You might be a little more polite, you know."

"Will-yum Grosh! You sure are tellin' me what to do today. I don't like it."

"Well, you better get used to it, for that's the way it is."

"That's what *I'm* afraid of."

Sleep would not come easily to Wilbur Bixby. It was bad enough having to bed down during the daylight hours, but now he couldn't shake the anger he felt about losing his best friend...well, his friend, anyway. And just because the captain liked this other fellow better! It wasn't fair! There would be the devil to pay now, and he, Wilbur, was just the one to give Old Scratch his due. He'd even the score somehow, if it took the entire voyage to do it. That young whippersnapper would learn a lesson he'd never forget. Yes, indeed. A grievous lesson it would be. He began to smile and to sink into the satisfied slumber of a man, if not with a plan, at least with a purpose.

CHAPTER 23
DECEPTION!

St. Louis, Missouri, 1 July, 1846

Charles Dickens wrote that, though it might improve in a few years, St. Louis was a town "not likely ever to vie, in point of elegance or beauty, with Cincinnati." He had roamed the narrow streets of the old French quarter of the town and noted the quaint wooden houses with their "tumble-down galleries before the windows, approachable by stairs or ladders from the streets." The pubs, the shops, the warehouses along the wharf, failed to impress him, but his hotel, which offered a luxurious meal, did.

The riverfront view of the town certainly impressed Philip as the Atta Boy pulled up to the wharf. The towering dome of the St. Louis Circuit Courthouse, the six-story City Hospital, the tall spire of St. Joseph's Church, the imposing bulk of the newly constructed Mercantile Library, the many brick edifices that painted a picture of a thriving industrial and commercial metropolis competed favorably, in Philip's view, with that "Porkopolis" of the Ohio river, Cincinnati.

When Philip climbed the stairs to the pilot house, he was surprised to see the first mate, Wilbur Bixby, at the wheel instead of Captain Grafton. Bixby was usually off duty by this time of the morning, snoring away noisily in his bunk. But it was Bixby who was docking the tugboat, yelling at the roustabouts to pull this haulyard or secure that line. Knowing of Bixby's antagonism toward him, Philip steeled himself and uttered, "Reporting for duty, Sir," a tinge of irony barely discernible in the phrasing of "Sir."

"Oh, it's you, Grosh. Cap'n Grafton's taken sick this morning. I'll be piloting once we're off again. I'm not partial to seein' your sorry butt on my bridge."

"I apologize, but Captain Grafton has me studying the piloting."

"Not on my watch, you're not. Say, there's a bit of a layover here in St. Looey while we wait for cargo. Just enough time for you to run an errand for the Cap'n."

"What's that, Sir?"

"Cap'n Grafton told me to have you take some papers over to the Steamboat Authority Office while we're docked here."

"Oh? What kind of papers?"

"That's not your concern. Registry papers, I think, though. Hang on a minute, I'll get them."

Wilbur Bixby ducked down the stairs into the officers' quarters and reappeared moments later with a bundle wrapped in brown paper. This he thrust into Philip's hands.

"Go to the office on Market Street. It's up about 10 blocks. You can't miss it. Ask for Mr. Casey. Hand it directly to him. Be back here by noon. Now be off with ya!"

Philip was just as glad to be out of Bixby's sight as Bixby was to be rid of Philip. A walk through a big city would be a pleasure after all the time he'd spent on water: stepping on ground that didn't move under his feet and knowing, more or less, which way was north or south, would be a welcome change. He stopped by his bunk and scooped a few coins and paper money from his kit bag. Perhaps he'd find a souvenir to purchase. Something for his mother. He'd have plenty of time to browse among the shops before noontime came.

Horse-drawn wagons brimming with every manner of goods and men on foot carrying huge bundles on their backs cluttered the quay as Philip stepped from the deck of the Atta Boy. Every nationality that Philip could identify, and many he could not, seemed to be represented in the throng. Asian men and women, dark-skinned men wearing turbans, Irishmen, Swedes, Germans, women with babies, blacks who were obviously slaves (the freed blacks would not leave the steamboats at the port of St. Louis, as they were immediately considered slaves once they set foot in Missouri), ragged street urchins running amongst the bustling crowd: all these emitted a kind of psychic energy that was intoxicating to a young man like Philip from a small country village.

He wandered into town and at once found Market Street. This he followed and soon found himself opposite the domed courthouse where, he remembered, a slave market was held on its very steps. As Philip stood pondering this awful reality, he saw a group of youths attack an older man on the courthouse lawn. The man grappled with the youths, then managed to scramble away. The young hooligans pursued him, yelling vicious obscenities. A battered placard lay in the dirt. Philip bent over this and read the painted words: "Free Dred and Harriet Scott!" As he puzzled over this curious sign and the resultant confrontation, a man approached from behind. "Damn abolitionists don't never learn!" said the man.

"I'm sorry, what did you say?" asked Philip.

"Abolitionists! All the time trying to free the coloreds."

"This Dred Scott, who is he?"

"Him and his wife is suing...suing, would you believe it? ...to get their freedom. Seems they lived in Illinois for a time. So what, I say. They's in Missourah now! Ain't you heared of this?"

"I'm new here. Not up on the current events. Sorry."

"Damn abolitionists," said the man, as he walked away, leaving Philip to stare alternately at the sign, then at the steps of the courthouse. He continued up Market street, dismayed by the hatred and intolerance he had just witnessed.

At last, Philip came to a two-story brick building on the west end of the town. A dark green paper window shade concealed the interior of the first floor office. A stained and cobwebbed sign proclaimed this to be the Steamboat Authority, but the office, like the neighborhood, seemed abandoned. A few feral cats fighting in the adjoining alley were the only sign of life. Philip knocked, then pounded on the door with his fists, unwilling to be stymied in his task. After many minutes of this, at which time his knuckles were quite bruised, the shade was pulled aside and a face that might have belonged to a pug dog, rather than a man, peered out. Teeth bared, the face snarled, "What is all the noise for?"

"Please, I'm delivering an important package. Open up!"

The man slowly opened the door but stood defiantly, blocking the entrance. Although Philip towered above him in height, the man's determined stance effectively discouraged Philip's forward progress.

"Is Mr. Casey about? I'm to place this into his hands."

"Casey? There's no Casey. Never been no Casey. This office's been closed for the last two years, lad. I'm just the caretaker. Can't imagine why anyone's ta want a package sent here."

"Closed? But there must be some mistake! Has the Authority moved?"

"Nope. Just shut down. Permanently. I thought that everybody knew."

"Hmm. Perhaps they did," said Philip, ripping open the brown paper wrapper to expose the contents of the package. Inside he found several folded sheets of last week's newspaper."

"Hey," said the pug-faced man, "is this some kind of joke?"

"It is," answered Philip. "And the joke's on me!"

Captain Absalom Grafton entered the pilothouse where First Mate Bixby sat in a wooden chair, his feet propped upon a window ledge, his hands locked behind his head, a small pipe protruding from his lips.

"Bixby! Why are we docked at St. Louis? This isn't our port of call."

"Sir, we was flagged down. They want us to carry the mail pouch up to Quincy. I think they thought we was the Bellflower. She's got the contract. I told 'em we doesn't have no contract to haul mail."

"Of course we don't! Get us away from here, Bixby. Cast off. We haven't time to lollygag around."

"Yes, Sir! Right away!"

"Where's young Philip?"

"I don't know, Cap'n, I ain't seen him this morning."

"Well, get to it!"

Bixby had kept a head of steam up as they sat in port and so the Atta Boy was able to get under way in a matter of minutes. Its bell clanging and the traditional black smoke pouring out of its funnel, she pulled into the channel and headed up the muddy river. By the time Philip rushed back to the wharf, she was gone.

"Look, Emma," said Elizabeth, pointing to the opposite shore as they passed by the city of St. Louis. "A pioneer family. See, that's how people travel west over land." A Conestoga wagon and two oxen sat along the river bank where a family had made a camp fire. They could see a man in a wide brimmed hat pointing at them, perhaps exclaiming with some amazement to his wife and children about the nature of this new technology of travel—the steamboat.

William had found a wide plank at one of the stops they had made to acquire wood for the boiler. He had rigged up a sort of walkway between the two flatboats, precarious when the river lapped against the boats and swung them to and fro, but still safer than the previous route Catherine Tennis had taken along the tow rope. The disadvantage of this construction was that the bridge afforded an irresistible challenge to the three-year-old Katy, who immediately tried to scamper across it. Will had grabbed her around the waist, saying, "No, no, little one! You're not allowed on that." But he found he needed to maintain a constant vigil against the little one's adventurous spirit. He pulled the plank in when he wasn't able to watch over it or when Cathy Tennis had come to visit. His mother, Catherine, had given him a scathing tongue lashing about the enterprise, but Will felt it was worth while to brave her anger, as that red-headed girl provided such a spark of happiness when she was around.

Philip stood on the levee, dumbfounded and angered at his own naiveté. "How am I ever going to catch that tug?" he said, not realizing he had spoken out loud.

"Excuse me, are you addressing me. Sir?" said a man standing next to him.

"I'm sorry. I didn't think..."

"Have you missed your boat, then?"

"My whole family is on it, not knowing I'm standing here on the dock."

"That's a sad circumstance. Where are they headed?"

"Up river."

"Will they be stopping at Clarksville or Louisiana?"

"I doubt it. I think maybe only at Hannibal. There's a load of coal going there."

"Well, then, you can catch 'em at Hannibal."

"They've a head start. Maybe an hour, maybe two, I don't know for sure."

"Ah, lad, but you'll go over land, ya see. On the river they've to wind back and forth and ease past islands. Take 'em a couple days to get to Hannibal. Overland is quicker. Ya go inna straight line. On a horse."

"Where am I going to get a horse?"

"Aye, that's the problem, ain't it?"

CHAPTER 24
ROLLIN' ON THE RIVER

Hannibal, Missouri, 3 July, 1846

It was a quiet little town, few people out and about. A bedraggled hound dog sniffed his way through the dust and dirt on Water Street, pausing to consider the nutritional value of a drifting scrap of paper, previously the wrapper around a sandwich of pork belly and pickles. An old man leaned against the livery stable, one leg bent so his foot braced him against the wall. He spit tobacco juice into the dust, accurately hitting the very same spot with each expectoration.

Philip led the horse up to the livery. It was a sad looking nag, sway-backed, covered with scabs where horse flies had chewed and thorns had scraped. The horse had cost Philip every cent he had but it had managed to get him to Hannibal without collapsing along the way. Philip entreated the stable man to take the horse, not hoping to sell him. He was more afraid the man would want money from Philip, money he no longer had.

"That's as sorry lookin' a piece of horse flesh as I ever seen," said the man. "Looks ready for the glue factory, if you ask me."

"You'll take him? Be kind to him. He just needs a good watering. A little food. He'll be right as rain. A good draft horse, you'll see."

"Oh, is he now? Well, I'd be hornswoggled ta take 'im, but I sees yer desperate to be rid of him. Road him hard, did ya?"

"No, sir, but he's a good old horse, real steady."

"Well, I caint give ya anything' fer him. But I'll take him and probably be able to find some use for 'im."

"Can you direct me to the wharf, sir?"

"Oh, sure. Just down the hill a piece. See the river past those trees there? Good travelin' to you, and thanks for the horse."

A boy sat on the stone levee, a fishing pole dangling from his hands, its tip dipping in and out of the river. He wore a battered straw hat with large chunks missing from the brim and he chewed on a long blade of grass. When he saw Philip approach he nodded with less than heartfelt enthusiasm and returned to studying the cork bobber which floated before him.

"Son, has there been a tug boat pulling a barge and two flats through here recently?"

"Naw. Nothin' but the daily packets. Not a good paddle wheeler in days come up or down. Wish they would, though."

"You like boats, boy?"

"Oh, yes sir. I'm going to run away one of these days and get a job as a steamboatman."

"I was a deckhand on the Messenger for a while. That's a pretty good sized steamboat."

"Ain't never heard of it, but I'll take your word for it. I'd really like to be a pilot, though. Tried to build a raft once. Dang thing sunk on me."

"Well, I'm trying to meet up with a tugboat that's pulling a couple flatboats. My family is on one of them."

"You'll see it come 'round the point from here. Too bad you ain't got a fishin' rod. Could make yourself one out of a branch off that cottonwood tree over yonder. I've a bit of extra string and hook. Worms in that can."

"An excellent idea. What's your name, son?"

"Sam. Sam Clemens, sir. Born and raised here and 'spect I'll die here 'fore I ever get on that river!"

William Tennis loved to entertain his family by playing the violin. His wife, Delila, was from Virginia, and William had learned some fiddle tunes from her Uncle Elias. One of these was called "The Rattlin' Bog," an old tune of Scottish origins about a tree growing in a bog. The children sang along as the verses progressed through its many variations:

"and on that tree there grew a limb...and on that limb there
was a nest...and in that nest there sat a bird..." and so on,
right down to the flea on the bird's feather. The Tennis
children were growing up in an environment rich in
traditional music and they danced with delight at the
chorus.

Hi-ho the rattlin' bog and the bog down in the valley-o
Hi-ho the rattlin' bog and the bog down in the valley-o

Will and Elizabeth had ventured across the makeshift
bridge to the Tennis flatboat and sat clapping as they
watched the five sisters, Cathy, Mary, Sarah, Susannah
and Delila, do-si-do in imitation of a Virginia Reel.
"The little one looks to be about Katy's age," said
Elizabeth. "I bet they'd like playing together."
"That's Delila. I think she's three. But you know we
can't let Katy on the plank. But maybe these people will be
our neighbors when we get to Illinois, though," said Will.
"You'd like that, wouldn't you. That red-headed girl,
especially! Why don't you get up and dance with her?"
"I can't dance! I'd look like an idiot."
"So what's so different about that?"

The Atta Boy slowed going through the tight chutes past
a series of islands just below Saverton. The river undulated
through the rocky landscape like a dying snake, coiling and
uncoiling. Islands formed where the river cut across those
coils, sometimes isolating a river town or devastating
farmland. Soon, the river widened again and the steamboat
glided along the muddy waterway toward Hannibal.

The cork bobbed, the line grew taught, and Philip knew
he had hooked something: a channel catfish, or an old
shoe, it didn't matter which—the sport was the thing. He
jerked up with his tree branch pole but the line snapped
and he fell backwards against the river bank.
"Aw, too bad," said Sam. "That was my last hook, too."
"Well, your line was kind of light for a fish that size, you
know."
"Ya. Must have been old Brutus. Brutus is a catfish, fifty

years old, and folks says he's maybe 15 feet long and weighs in at about 200 pounds. I hooked him once and he dragged me half way to Quincy 'fore I had to let him go. Out of kindness, it was. Just couldn't cut short that old fella's life."

"Yes, or it was that sunken tree limb I can see peeking up over by where my bobber is floating."

"Say, Mr. Grosh, I think I see your steamboat comin' up the river. See over there 'round the point?"

"It does look like the Atta Boy. I'd better hurry down to the wharf to meet her."

"Well, good luck with that. She's not dockin' here. She'll go right past."

"What? How do you know that?"

"See, she's on the island side of the river, in the wrong channel to be coming into port. Besides, there's no black smoke. They always put pine tar on the fire to make the smoke black when they come to land. Signals to the local folks to meet her. Her smoke is white. She'll pass by. Sorry."

"I have to get out to her. How can I do that? Is there a boat I can borrow?"

"Well, I'm not saying there is and I'm not saying there isn't, but if we was to borrow my Uncle Joe's skiff, and rowed out real fast into the middle, we might just meet her 'fore she goes by."

"Could we get her to stop to pick me up?"

"Well, that depends on whether they care if they plow right over a small boat or not. Course, they may not see us, either."

Captain Absalom Grafton pulled the chain that sent a blast of heated air through the steamboat's horn. "Damn fools! What do they think they're doing?" he exclaimed, cursing the small boat and the man and boy in it who had appeared directly in the Atta Boy's path. "We'll hit 'em for sure!" He swung the wheel violently toward larboard and yelled the "all stop" through the speaking tube that ran down to the engine room. This he followed with an "all reverse full," the steamboat staggered to a halt mere feet from the skiff that Philip and Sam Clemens had maneuvered so recklessly in front of it. Philip stood and waved his arms.

"What the... is that young Philip? You dang fool! Get out of my way!" yelled the captain. The Atta Boy was "jack knifing," swinging around perpendicular to the river, while its towed cargo, the barge and flatboats, continued forward, angling toward the island on their right. Sam and Philip rowed around the bow of the steamboat and threw a line up to a roustabout who hung over the rail. The roustabout was shaking his fist at them and failed to catch the line.

"Secure that skiff, ya lubber," ordered Captain Grafton. After a second throw, the small boat was tethered to the side of the Atta Boy and a rope ladder was thrown over the side. Philip mounted this, unsure of the nature of greeting he would receive from the angered tugboat captain and crew. He found out, all too soon, that it might have been more prudent to have remained in his "disappeared" status. Captain Grafton harangued Philip for what seemed like hours, as the boat straightened and slowly resumed its course up river. Sam Clemens had returned to the shore and his fishing pole, hoping to hook old Brutus one more time.

The flatboats had been jostled and the plank bridge had fallen into the water. This might have stranded William and Elizabeth on the Tennis' boat, had not the two flatboats come together with a loud bang, allowing the Grosh children to hop safely across to their own boat. Being more or less the caboose of the water bound train, they were unaware of what or who had caused the sudden collision. They were happy simply to still be afloat and moving in the right direction.

Finally the captain's wrath subsided and Philip got a word in edgewise. It was Bixby that had tricked him into getting off the boat, he told Grafton. Bixby who had left without him. He was truly sorry about blocking the Atta Boy in the channel, but he had to gain access to the tug boat in order to tell his story. He didn't know what to expect, except that he knew the captain was an honest man, and that the first mate was not. He had come back, he said, because he also felt he owed the captain his loyalty and his labor in payment for towing the flatboat up the river. He would steer clear of Bixby, as much as that was possible, he said, for the remainder of the trip to Savanna.

Captain Grafton ruminated upon Philip's explanation, considering what he knew about the young man's enthusiasm and dedication to learning about river navigation, about the industrious attitude he had for hard work. He compared this to what he knew about Wilbur Bixby, about his lassitude and apathy, the slothfulness with which he performed his job. He knew Bixby to be more than capable of jealousy and wasn't surprised at the devious method Philip alleged the first mate had used to eliminate his rival. Still, the dangerous stunt he had pulled weighed against him. Could he trust the riverboat to such a reckless fellow?

"I tell you what," said Captain Grafton, after a few moments of contemplation, "I'll keep you on up to Savanna. I was meaning to induce you to stay with the boat, become a cub pilot under my tutelage, but now I think your destiny is elsewhere. Perhaps farming is your future, as opposed to a career on the river. However, I do believe you. You was snookered by a rat bastard, but one that would never endanger the ship."

And so it was that Philip never became a riverboat pilot, and that was just as well, for it wasn't in his blood, the way it was with others. Others, like the young boy that had fished with him and helped to stop a paddlewheel steamboat in the middle of the Mississippi river.

CHAPTER 25
EXODUS FROM NAUVOO

Nauvoo, Illinois, 4 July, 1846

Once past Hannibal Captain Grafton had mellowed somewhat and again took Philip under his wing.

"I guess I never told you about the Majestic. That was the wreck we passed when you were starting to learn piloting."

"No, Sir, I don't recall that you did."

"It be a cautionary tale for you to hear about the endangering of a steamboat through negligence. They say there's no such thing as an accident—that may indeed be true. Well, you see, there was a young deckhand on the Ole Miss—that was the boat. And...oh, the Ole Miss, she was a grand example of riverboat extravagance: all brick-a-brack and gingerbread. She lured one into overconfidence with all that decorative aplomb, the gilded arrogance that she displayed. The young deckhand thought she was a rich palace fit for kings and princes, a fortress impervious to the destructive forces of nature...or of man.

"He was on watch that morning. There was a fog upon the river and the Ole Miss was keeping toward the shore line so she could see it clear enough not to run aground. One could always imagine themselves to be safely in the middle of the river when they're not—for fog, she plays tricks on even the most experienced pilot. So the young deckhand was stationed on the bow and a snag boat was out front with lanterns to signal the way.

"If an obstruction was found, the snag boat would place a lighted buoy—really just a weighted piece of wood with a lantern hung atop it—where the rock or reef or sunken limb was. The man on watch would then signal the pilot, that is, if he were doing his job. Well, that morning the young deckhand was hung over. He'd been three sheets to the wind the night before, celebratin' back in port 'til the early hours and drunk as a skunk when he returned to the boat. He felt he had a perfect excuse to nod off a bit, as that place in the river had never turned dangerous and he knew the pilot knew it well.

"He never saw the lighted buoy nor did he signal the pilot. The buoy was set wrong and it tipped, extinguishing the lantern. The Ole Miss plowed into the reef with such force her bottom was ripped asunder and her side paddles splintered into toothpicks. She hung on the reef for a few minutes, then she broke into two parts and slid off the reef into deep water where she lies to this day.

"Forty people died that morning. Most got to safety, including the young deckhand who blamed himself, and rightly so. He never drank again. And now you know why I'm so hard on you when you pull a stunt like you did today."

"You said you saw her go down," said Philip.

"Aye, I did. You see, I was that young deckhand."

John Grosh stood looking out at the Mississippi. So much water, he thought, and how different it can be. There is the water of tranquility when the river is calm, the surface smooth as glass and spotted with the shining reflections of clouds. Then comes a subtle boiling that obscures and distorts those puffs of white, bringing a gray green tint up through the muddy brown depths. Ripples may form, as if some giant hand is shaking the river banks, ever so slightly.

There is the water of discontent when the river shrugs its shoulders at the intrusion of an uninvited entity, a fallen tree, a riverboat. It surges to and fro, it froths, it complains and then, if it is unable to vanquish the interloper, to cover it or consume it, it simply parts and splashes around it. This water's colors are many and varied, punctuated by sparkles of silver and of gold.

There is the water of deceit, which falsifies its depth or hides the wreckage of another voyager who misread its message. This water is opaque and colorless. There is angry water, furious at the restriction of its channels, rumbling over rocks or forming eddies, whirling and hurtling and tearing at the land. It is flecked with white. There is fast water, slow water, water that seems to move in all directions at once, water so clear it disappears, water so impenetrable it seems solid. Water that is alive, churning with algae, sprouting reeds and cattails. Water that is dead, black and brackish, lapping against the rotting roots of trees, with the flotsam of decaying fish in its dire soup.

Water that becomes a carpet of bright colors when springtime blossoms drop. Water of somber shades of orange and brown when fall leaves are shed. Water stippled by driblets of gentle rain or lathered by a deluge. Ornamented with ever expanding circles where sunfish pluck water striders from its surface. Littered with the jetsam of passing steamboats. Dirtied by the coal dust and debris of an industrial revolution. Slipping through fingers and leaving only grit or slush.

Water frozen, crystalline, dusted with winter's contribution of powered moisture, marked by the pads of wolves or the boots of man, cracking with a noise like thunder, holding at bay the advance of the boats of man. Water, in all its myriad forms, strong enough to break rocks and wash away whole towns, yet soft, flowing, vibrant and vital—this was the river that John saw before him, the river whose path he followed, the river that had brought their party to the troubled town of Nauvoo, Illinois.

Nauvoo! A small river town once called Commerce, was renamed by Joseph Smith, Jr., then the leader of a new religion, the Latter Day Saints, or Mormons. The Mormons, building a "New Zion" in Jackson County, Missouri, were considered fanatics and an economic threat by the non-Mormon settlers. They were forced out of Missouri in what came to be called the 1838 Mormon War. They fled to Illinois. At first, opinion was in their favor and a distain for their treatment by the Government of Missouri prompted the citizens of Illinois to support them in their quest for a permanent home. They purchased land in the town of Commerce, and called it "Nauvoo," which means "Beautiful City."

The Mormons swelled their city to a population rivaling nearby Quincy and Springfield. A spectacular temple began to rise on a hill high above the town. Smith became president of the church, mayor of the town and head of the Mormon militia, giving him enormous power and influence. But there was trouble in paradise. Smith had begun to practice polygamy and advocated plural marriages by the church's congregation. This and the growing political power of the Mormons began to foster hostilities among non-Mormons in the neighboring communities. Another war began. A detractor within the Mormon Church, William Law, had been excommunicated and began his own church and a newspaper with which he denounced Smith. Smith marched into the newspaper office with his militia and destroyed the press. Smith was arrested (for polygamy as well as the abuse of power) and held for trial in Carthage, when an angry mob stormed the jail and shot Smith and his brother, killing them. Hostilities toward the Mormons escalated.

By the end of 1845, the new leader of the Church of Latter Day Saints, Brigham Young, saw that his church would never survive persecution in these United States and decided on an exodus to the western territory where they could at last found their "New Zion" in peace and without interference. In February of 1846, when the river was frozen, over two thousand Mormons began the trek to Utah, where they would eventually settle. By the time Isaac and his family reached Nauvoo, many Mormons had left, but the exodus was still continuing in what must have seemed like a steady stream of people being ferried across the Mississippi to Iowa.

While the Atta Boy was stopped at Nauvoo, John strolled along the levee. He could feel tension in the air. They had heard something about the Mormon conflicts even back in Pennsylvania, but seeing the exodus first hand was eye opening. There were two distinct groups of people present and they each made known their strong opinions. Sharp words were exchanged between bystanders and the Mormons with their wagons full of household goods, their children and their wives.

John sidled up to a man chewing on what appeared to some kind of pie, who watched, but did not participate in the ongoing mutual harangue. Other than the pie, there was little to distinguish the man from the milling crowd. A dispassionate demeanor was his only unique feature. John couldn't help engaging this man in conversation, as his curiosity about the hubbub on the levee was piqued.

"Fruit or meat?" John inquired.

"Meat, and delicious! There's a pie stand up the street if you're hungry."

"I may investigate that. Thank you. Say, there's quite a bit of activity on this wharf today."

"Not so much different from usual. You're not from here abouts, are you?"

"A traveler. I understand the Mormons are in some turmoil?"

"You would say so. Now, I'm more or less neutral in the matter, but there's some that takes it upon themselves to help the tribe on their way out of town. They aren't above lighting a fire under them, you might say."

"A fire?"

"A few of the houses got burned. It's the kind of thing happens when people gets scared of another group. That Smith character got himself killed. Kind of signaled the go ahead to some of the intolerant types."

"Religious intolerance? There's plenty of history for that."

"Maybe I can give you a bit of perspective, though. Have you ever heard of a man named Dan Rice?"

"Rice? Sounds familiar, but I'm not sure..."

"Has a circus now. Interesting fellow. A showman, started out as a strong man. See, he could have a heavy slab of rock placed on his chest and broken with a sledge hammer, or he could bend a steel rod. Did tricks with horses trying in vain to pull him off a bench, things like that. So back when Smith was the prophet, as he called himself, Dan Rice showed up styling himself as a preacher. He saw an opportunity for bleeding the congregation dry of its money by being more miraculous than the miracle worker, Mr. Smith.

"Smith saw his act and took him on, pretending that

Rice got his strength and abilities from God, via Smith, of course. They was both in the business of duping other people, you see. But Rice and Smith argued about how much money Rice was worth and Rice took off to Iowa, across the river. He developed a hatred of Smith and desired to expose him for the fraud he knew him to be. You know, it takes one to know one.

"About this time, Smith needed another miracle to rally his faithful followers, and he hit on an idea that actually had been Rice's. He announced he would walk on the water on such and such a date. Before this he prepared the illusion by placing some long planks of wood just beneath the surface of the river where no one would notice them. He would walk on the planks, and from the shore, it would appear he was walking on top of the water.

"Rice got wind of the scam and the night before Smith's miracle, he ventured forth in a small boat and removed a section of the planks, out, maybe thirty feet from shore where Smith would be walking, confident that his trick was working. The assembled crowd gasped in awe as Smith ambled out across the surface of the muddy Mississippi, seemingly walking on water in the manner of the Savoir in the Bible. When he got to the section Rice had removed, he plunged into the depths of the river. You could hear the cries of the crowd, and, had you been in the right place, the laughter of Dan Rice."

"That's quite a story," said John. "But most religions have some kind of hocus pocus going on. These people must be real believers to uproot their families and take to the wilderness like they're doing."

"Well, when you get chased out of several places, you tend to get to lookin' far a field for succor. It's like Moses in the Bible, I guess."

"I guess. Well, I believe I'll wander up the street and get one of those pies. It's been nice talking to you."

Up on the hill, the temple of the Mormons glistened in the sunlight, even as their minions marched down to the river, perhaps expecting it to part, like the Red Sea. The settlers of Western Illinois, having first chased off the Native Americans who dwelt there, had once again secured the land for themselves.

CHAPTER 26
SAMMY FUNK

Savanna, Illinois, 6 July, 1846

The river had taken on impossible proportions. It had widened into what appeared to be a broad lake sprinkled with dozens of small islands. It was a vast floodplain ranging across a sand prairie where numerous tributaries entered the river and herons strutted through the shallows. Finding the right channel through this watery labyrinth demanded an experienced pilot, and Captain Grafton was up to the challenge.

Eagles soared above them as they passed the confluence of the Maquoketa River with the Mississippi just above Green Island. They passed Brickhouse Slough where the Apple River entered the big river. Egrets and pelicans, sand darters and blue herons patrolled the marshes fishing for mussels and crabs among the wild celery beds. At the mouth of the Plum River lay the small river town of Savanna.

It was an auspicious landfall for the flatboat families. Savanna represented the terminus of their voyage, and nearly the end of their journey. Here the Atta Boy cut loose her passengers and turned south down river on her return trip. The flatboats were moored at the wharf, their inhabitants pensive, perhaps apprehensive at the prospect of leaving the soggy wooden platforms they had called home for months. The unpleasant aspects of life on the river had at least been a known quality. The unknown now loomed ahead of them.

Sam Funk had a small farm 40 miles east of Savanna, in the Pine Creek Township of Ogle County. He was tall and lanky and there was a swagger in his walk. He had sand colored hair and beard, and had inherited the aquiline nose of his ancestors. To say he was goodhearted was to understate his magnanimous nature. Sam had moved to Illinois with his wife, Barbara, in 1840. Together they had raised nine children, five boys and four girls. Barbara had died two years ago, leaving Sam searching for meaning in life. This he had found in aiding other pioneers from the east who desired to settle on the hearty and bountiful Illinois prairie.

Sam, or Sammy, as his friends called him, made frequent trips to Savanna, shuttling newcomers from the river port to the rolling prairie lands that were for sale. It was a coincidence that he arrived in Savanna the same day that Isaac left the flatboat to stroll through the small town looking for opportunity. But as fortuitous as it may have seemed, it was inevitable that the Grosh family would meet up with the Funks, if not this day, then another.

William Tennis had already negotiated for the sale of his flatboat and the purchase of a horse and wagon with which he could transport his family and their belongings across the prairie to a new home in Ogle County. As Isaac bartered to sell his boat, Sammy Funk saw and recognized him from earlier days when the Funks had lived for a time in Huntingdon in Pennsylvania. Delighted to be able to offer help to an old friend, he hailed Isaac at once.

"Isaac Grosh, you made it at last!" he called.

"Sammy! Is it you? This is wonderful! I was coming to find you but I wasn't sure where your farm was."

"Well luckily, I've found you. And I think you'll be pleased with the area. My farm's by Pine Creek. There is still land for sale near by. You'll have to clear it of rocks and some trees, but it's the best farm land in the world. You'll come and stay with me until you buy land and build a house—no argument, now."

"Well, let me just finish my transaction with this gentleman here. I'm selling the flatboat in order to buy a horse and wagon."

"Isaac, Isaac, Issac. You have no need for a wagon. All your family and your possessions will fit easily into mine. And that other family, the Tennises, they've got a wagon. And listen, you might want to keep the boat. Some folks take them apart and use the wood for their houses."

"Sammy, I've lived in that infernal box for so long now, I don't ever want to see a fiber of it again!"

"Ha! Okay then. I'll wait and we'll go down and fetch your family."

Catherine gave Sammy a bear hug when she saw him step down onto the flatboat. It wasn't that their families had been closer than any others in the Brethren community back home, it was just that Samuel Funk III was not only the first familiar face they'd seen in a long time, but he embodied stability and hope in a world that was suddenly upside down with uncertainty.

"How is your family? How is Barbara," she asked.

"Oh, you couldn't have known. Barbara passed away two years ago."

"I'm so sorry! Was she... was she ill?"

"It was the influenza. I was only glad that it missed the children."

"And your children? How are they doing?"

"Maria is married, of course, and George and Michael have their own farms. Peter is still with me, though not for long, I fear, as he is gaining his majority soon. Catherine and Isaac you might remember, as they were born before we came here. But our littlest one, our sweetheart, was born right here in Illinois. We called her Barbara, after her mother. She's 5 now."

"My goodness," said Catherine, "how time does go by! Well, here is my tribe. You remember Philip, our oldest, and John and William, of course. Here's James, he was only 8 when you left, but look how he's grown up!"

"Aw. Mother!" complained James.

"This young man over here is my nephew, Dick Cornelius. He'll be scouting out land for his family."

"Yes," said Sammy, "I know your father and mother. I'll be happy to help you find good land."

"Thank you sir," said Dick.

"And Mary Jane and Elizabeth," continued Catherine, "they're 12 and 10 now. And Emma is about the age of your Barbara..."

"I'm six, Mother!" said Emma.

"And our youngest, Katy—Catherine, I mean, is 3."

"Hello, girls, I'm happy to meet you. And this furry creature over here? What's his name?" asked Sammy.

"That's Lancelot," retorted Emma. "He's my dog!"

"Oh, your dog. I see. Yes. Your dog. Well, if you all want to start loading things into the wagon, I'll go see if the Tennis family would like to travel with us."

"Will we see any Indians?" asked James.

"Maybe. But only friendly ones now-a-days. Wasn't always that way, though."

"Oh boy, I bet you have some great stories..."

"Maybe another time, Jimmy. Maybe another time."

The little caravan took off later that afternoon, the Groshes and Sammy Funk in the lead wagon with the Tennis wagon following. The rolling hills and palisades gave way to a flattened prairie. The trail, marked by wagon ruts, weaved through tall grasses and wild flowers. Beebalm and silky aster competed with buffalo clover and dog-tooth violet for the attention of myriads of bees and butterflies. Rabbits scampered and quail ran erratically as the wagons rolled past their hamlets. The wagon wheels were clotted red from wild strawberries growing profusely in the ruts. The cluster of wooden houses near Savanna thinned and soon the travelers were surrounded by a vast expanse of greens and yellows and a silence broken only by wind and horses' hooves.

Sammy's wagon was covered with bleached muslin which flapped and ruffled in the wind. The Groshes sat inside this, perched on top of barrels and boxes of their worldly goods, brought so carefully along the rivers. Finally freed from the confines of their flatboat, it was ironic that they were crammed into the tiny quarters of this "prairie schooner," unable to experience the wondrous space surrounding them. When darkness forced the caravan to stop and make camp, the children burst from the wagon and ran wildly through the tall grass, collecting many a burr or pricker. Lancelot sprang and leaped as only a joyful canine can, thrilled to be once again on open land.

The women boiled dried beans in a huge iron kettle over the open campfire. Coffee and yes, corn bread; bacon which sizzled in a skillet and apple butter for the bread were enjoyed under a crepuscular sky bespeckled with twinkling stars. They couldn't remember a sky so immense, stretching endlessly, almost without a horizon. A sky so black yet filled with the brilliance of millions of spots of silvery light, the sparkling, diamond-like scintilla of an unimaginable cosmos.

After the meal, William Tennis brought out his violin and bowed an old fiddle tune. The younger children danced around the campfire in glee. Catherine Grosh and Delila Tennis sat together, watching the revelry.

"It's wonderful," said Catherine, "that our children can finally get a chance to play together. Even though our boats were attached by ropes, we were so separated during that trip up river."

"Well, we did get to know William pretty well," answered Delila.

James sat next to Sammy Funk. "Uncle Sammy," he called him, although they were not related. Dried logs crackled on the campfire before them, sending up fountains of sparks.

"Uncle Sammy, please tell me about the Indians."

"Well, young James, it's like I said, there isn't much to tell. The last hostilities were back in '32. The Blackhawk War."

"Wow! Blackhawk. He was a fierce Indian chief, wasn't he?"

"Blackhawk was the war chief. The Sauks and the Foxes were Indian tribes that Blackhawk led back into Illinois. See, there had been a treaty back then that wasn't all that fair. The Indians had to give up all their lands in Illinois and live west of the Mississippi. Blackhawk went up to the Winnebago village on the Rock River thinking all the other Indians would side with him.

"They didn't. In fact, some began helping the U.S. troupes and militiamen that were sent to control Blackhawk's band. Well, the story goes, Blackhawk was ready to return to Iowa with his people and he sent a message to the militiamen requesting to be allowed to cross the river. Only nobody spoke the Indians' language. The militia—and you need to know that these were not trained men, like the United States Army, no. They were mostly settlers who were first of all, irate that the Indians dared return to reclaim their lands, and second of all, mostly drunk and disorderly.

"The Federal troops were nowhere to be seen and so the militiamen attacked Blackhawk, which pretty much guaranteed that peaceful negotiations would be impossible. Blackhawk couldn't head west across the Mississippi without encountering militia so he moved up the Rock and into the Territory of Wisconsin. Besides Sauks and Foxes, he had some Winnebagoes, Kickapoos and Potawatomis with him and two other chiefs, Napope and White Cloud.

"There were raids on settlements and minor battles with Federal troops that went on for months with no real purpose or order to them. Sometimes the Indian attacks were made by groups not even associated with Blackhawk. It was chaos. Well, the fighting went on and the army chased Blackhawk up and down the Wisconsin River. The Indians were tired and starved and disillusioned whereas the army was well rested, well armed and outnumbered the Indians many times over.

"Eventually they reached the Mississippi and started to cross but reinforcements for the army had been sent up the river on a steamboat which arrived in time to open fire with an artillery piece. Blackhawk and White Cloud tried again to surrender but once again, their language could not be understood. Many were drowned or killed and Blackhawk's numbers dwindled.

"Then came the battle of Bad Axe, the worst of all for the Indians. It was slaughter. The soldiers fired at anybody who tried to swim across the river: men, women, children, women with babies on their backs, wounded Indians who would probably would have drowned anyway. The soldiers scalped many of the dead or cut strips of flesh from their backs to make razor straps. Nobody knows how many were killed, perhaps five hundred. It was a bad day for all concerned.

"Blackhawk and White Cloud and Napope had escaped to Wisconsin and were hidden out in the Winnebago and Ojibwa villages. But they still kept trying to surrender.

Finally they managed to do so. They were held in jail in St. Louis, but later sent east on a sort of tour. They were famous, and people clamored to see them. Baltimore, Philadelphia, New York City, Detroit. They were painted by famous artists and Blackhawk narrated an autobiography which was published. The were later released. Then the government went to the Winnebagoes and demanded they surrender all their lands in Illinois and Wisconsin and move west of the Mississippi. It was just another land grab based on the excuse that they had helped Blackhawk.

"So you see, young James, the Indian wars were never romantic, they were tragic beyond belief."

Sleeping under the stars in a sea of grass, the families were arranged in a circle around the fire which still cast a red glow of warmth onto their bare faces. Lancelot snuggled up to Emma, matching his breathing to hers. A moon, not nearly full, but waxing admirably, rose into the star filled sky. Off in the distance, a plaintive howling was too faint to heard by human ears. But the wolf pup perked up, sniffed the air, gave the sleeping girl the equivalent of a wolf kiss: the sticky tongue drawn wetly across the tender cheek. Up on his haunches, then bounding through the tall grass, his tail held straight out like a lance, the wolf pup followed the sound.

CHAPTER 27
LANCELOT

The Illinois Prairie, 7 July, 1846

The pale moon barely penetrated the tall prairie grass where the wolf pup pushed his way, his keen nose ferreting out a host of exciting smells, his good night vision nearly the match for the deep shadows, his perked ears focused on the distant singing of kindred creatures. The promise of family urged him on, yet instinctively, he knew what perils he faced. In his own brood the competition among siblings had been fierce. No outsider would have been tolerated. This was a strange new land where wolves were dominant—his nose told him that. Their markings were everywhere, and everywhere there was the sign of violent struggle: a rabbit, a prairie chicken, a partridge, and perhaps larger game that flattened the grass as it ran, leaped, bounded in a futile attempt to escape gaping mouths that ripped and tore at its haunches.

Dawn came before he reached the pack and its kill. He stood on a hillock overlooking a shallow depression in the landscape where the wolf pack milled around the carcass of a deer, its blood darkening the ground. A large wolf, most likely the pack's matriarch, rended the soft underbelly of the deer, devouring entrails, kidneys, and other delicacies, while the other wolves lay silently watching and waiting for their turn. Lancelot's scent had not yet reached the pack and so he watched and waited as well, determining the hierarchy of the group by observation of the wolves' body language and facial expressions.

There were two or three pups, about his age or younger, who nuzzled against a female and hung back from the rest. Near the kill a young male became restless and rose to approach the deer. The matriarch snarled and snapped at him and he quietly backed away, his ears held back, his tail drooping. Lancelot knew that introducing himself to the pack at this juncture could be suicidal. It would be better to wait until they had all eaten their fill and were resting. He turned and scampered down the opposite side of the hillock.

Once past the last scent of the pack's urine, and therefore out of their current territory, Lancelot set out to hunt. The sight of the deer had awakened his own hunger. For too long he had fed on ruined food given him by the two-legs. For some reason they chose to burn their meat, rendering it bloodless and dry. It was time to feel his teeth sink into the soft, writhing body of bird or rabbit. To hear the crunch of bones and the squeal of a dying animal. Perhaps the stream he had jumped had some tasty fish in it. Nose to the ground, he ventured once again into the tall grass.

It was easy for him to decipher the prairie. The dense bundles of tall wheatgrass provided protection for rabbits' warrens and ground-nesting birds. Clusters of black-eyed Susans attracted flying insects who were a meal for wrens and cardinals, difficult birds to catch, but good sport. There were few trees, but the occasional stand of oak or walnut was home to red squirrels which required stealth and speed to conquer. He found a nest in the grass and enjoyed an appetizer of quail eggs.

For a wolf pup who had had little exercise in the past month the chase was exhilarating. He found himself at the base of trees watching squirrels chattering at him from the heights. He abandoned this enterprise and dug down into a prairie dog hole until he finally realized his prey had escaped through a back door. Some of the lessons he had learned from his mother were coming back to him. Once identified, the prey must be slowly and quietly crept upon, shortening the distance for the chase. Some of these critters were darn fast!

At last he brought down a rabbit and consumed each morsel with relish. He found a stream and plunged into its cool freshness, washing the remaining scent of humans from his fur. He was no longer a dog—he was wolf again.

But wolves are social animals, needing the pack for support and for structure. So he returned to the hillock where he could look down at the deer kill. The wolf pack was gone. Above in the sky circled turkey vultures and crows. At the carcass sat a lone coyote, feasting on what little remained of the deer.

Lancelot ambled down the hillock and confronted the coyote. The coyote reared back and snarled, showing teeth dripping with blood and bits of flesh. Lancelot took his most ferocious stance, bristled the fur on his back and let out a low howl. He curled back his lips showing his own glistening teeth and began inching toward the coyote. With a yip and a yelp the animal turned tail and ran. A lone coyote was no problem. He just hoped it didn't return with its brothers and sisters.

Lancelot latched onto the rear leg of the deer carcass with his teeth and tugged and twisted until he had pulled it off at the joint. Proudly he dragged his prize away from the kill and into a wooded area, the bulk of the leg weighing more than he did. In the woods he chewed on stringy venison and cracked open bone to lap up the marrow. Satiated, he slept for a while before resuming his tracking of the wolf pack.

He followed the pack for another day before he dared make contact, observing and learning the rules the family followed. He kept down wind and out of sight but felt the pack knew of his presence by some wolf sense that couldn't be explained. The following day he saw his opportunity when the mother and her pups lay in the shade of a mulberry bush, mother watchful as the pups played wolf pup games, designed to temper their aggressive natures. He eased into the play and was surprised not to be rejected by the pups. He was a little older and larger, stronger and more skilled at the rough and tumble activity and occasionally had to correct one of the pups who bit or pulled too hard. The mother lay still, watching. At any moment, Lancelot knew, she might rear up and attack to drive him off. But perhaps his tutelage of her litter impressed her favorably. For now, he was safe.

One of the younger males saw him and strolled over to sniff the interloper. Lancelot flopped down and rolled to expose his belly in the classic submissive pose that wolves use under such circumstances. This seemed to placate the male—for the moment. But a second male joined them bringing a less than docile attitude into the investigation of the newcomer. This wolf didn't like what he saw and began a low, rumbling growl that set the hackles up on Lancelot's back. He rose and started to back away from the aggressive male who in turn followed, teeth bared and tail carried high. It was just a matter of time before the male would leap and clasp his jaws around Lancelot's throat. But the mother rose and butted the male with her head. Her expression spoke with the authority of a dominant female, an authority not to be questioned or challenged, at least not by a young wolf who risked being driven from the pack for insubordinate behavior.

By now all the other wolves were gathered around watching. Some, no doubt, were anxious to see a blood-letting. The large alpha female, the one that had orchestrated the feeding order back at the deer carcass, approached Lancelot. Again, the wolf pup flopped and rolled, submissive and hoping against hope not to have his throat torn open. Minutes went by as the alpha female poked and sniffed with her bulbous nose. She seemed to be thinking, considering—her eyes narrowed to slits and her mouth slowly opened, saliva dripping. Then all at once her enormous tongue extended and she licked Lancelot across the muzzle. He had been accepted into the wolf pack!

As Lancelot was finding a new family, the families of Isaac Grosh and William Tennis rolled their wagons onto the Samuel Funk farm at Pine Creek. Sammy now had to take care of a few house guests in addition to running his farm, but the extra work didn't fazed at all. In fact, he loved the energy of the children and knew that the older boys and girls would roll up their sleeves to help. The new pioneers took to the countryside at once, admiring the rich soil, the level land, the flowing creeks that brought water to the crops, and the wooded hills where lumber was abundant. Game was plentiful, Sammy told them, There were fish in the streams and wild fowl, even deer and elk that wandered down onto their lands.

There was much to do: The land agent needed to be contacted, land looked at, arrangements for tools, seed, animals, the building of a house, the plowing and cultivating of fields in anticipation of next year's spring planting. There was a fellow down at Grand Junction, Sammy told them, a blacksmith named Deere who made the most amazing plows. Those old iron ones from back east, he explained, were no good here. The dirt just stuck to them and needed to be cleaned off every few feet. Some folks were ready to go back east because of it, but this fellow Deere, Sammy said, had invented a self-cleaning plow made of polished steel. Worked like a charm.

"But first," said Sammy, "we shall celebrate!" Sammy sent his son, Peter, to the farms of his two eldest sons, George and Michael. "Tell them to come," he said, "bring their families and bring their instruments!" And soon, as a pig roasted on a spit and corn boiled in a kettle, music was heard on the Funk farm.

CHAPTER 28
ISAAC WALKS THE LAND

Pinecreek Township, 12 July, 1846

"Things wasn't settled for sure with the Indians until after the Treaty of Chicago was ratified. The one after the Blackhawk War, not the one before it. White people had settled here and there and a couple big companies was buying land from the Indians in large quantities—the Illinois an' Wabash Company, it was—but the British refused to recognize they could buy from the natives and after Illinois became a state in '18, they got unrecognized again. So you gotta buy from the government, or find somebody ready to sell. Funny though, the Indians never thought you could actually own land. They were just custodians of it, they said."

Sammy Funk continued his dissertation on Pine Creek Township history as the wagon rattled along the dirt tracks that served for roads. Beside him on the worn wooden bench seat sat Isaac Grosh and Dick Cornelius, eager to inspect the virgin prairie where land could be purchased for farming. The sun shone brilliantly in the cloudless July sky and the prairie winds sang through pine needles in the thick woods along the creek.

"I guess old man Baker was one of the first. Put up a log house in '34, up here where there is timber and a good spring and a view out across the rolling prairie. So from here we go over those low hills and across the flatter land where I think you might like to locate."

"Still some timber along here," commented Isaac.

"Yes, but it gives way to prairie on the west side. You could clear what you need and have lumber for building. But make sure you have a spring or access to a creek."

"Is there a town around here?" asked Dick Cornelius.

"There is Oregon to the east of us and Mount Morris north. Polo to the west. A half day's travel," answered Sammy Funk, bouncing up and down on the wagon bench as the wheels rolled over rocks and the hardened dirt of wagon ruts. A mocking bird began a recital of the forged songs of a dozen other birds, summoning the wayfarers toward their goal. The land, rarely trodden upon by hoof, paw or foot, lay open and inviting, its promise: to reveal the wonders of its natural fertility to those who would nurture it.

They reached a place along a small stream where the land sloped gently away from a thick woods. It leveled out and bristled with tall grass and wild flowers, seeming to stretch endlessly toward the horizon. The cheeping of frogs in the stream was answered by the chirping of grasshoppers in the field as if a contest existed to determine who could complain the loudest about the human interlopers.

Isaac felt a sense of tranquility here. Yet he visualized the potential of this magnificent terrain: he saw crops swaying where Indian grass and bluestem now waved. In his mind's eye he superimposed his father's farm over this undeveloped land. Here was the barn, there the corral. Pigs rooted and chickens ran free, pecking at the dirt. Wheat grew tall and golden, glistening in the sun. "Let's get out and walk a bit," he said. Sammy Funk reined up the horse and the three descended to the savanna.

Isaac reached down and pulled a handful of tall grass out of the ground. The rich loam clung to the roots so that the clod resembled a dark brown sea anemone, tentacles stilled from the shock of a changed environment. He scooped dirt from the hole and rubbed it between his palms. "Good earth," he remarked. He could smell the freshness of minerals mixed with the tang of decay. The granules coated his fingers, stuck under his nails. He tasted it: he tasted youth, innocence, hope. He knew he was in a special place. "This is it," he said. "This will be my future."

Dick Cornelius looked around. As far as he could see in any direction there was...nothing. "For my way of thinking," he said, "this place is the middle of nowhere. It's desolate, lonely, empty. There are no people to be seen for miles around."

"There will be people, Dick," said Sammy. "More are coming. From Pennsylvania. Brethren. Our people. Now is the time to grab up this land before it's all taken."

"But it feels...it feels as if no human being has ever walked here. It's primeval." With that Dick kicked at the ground dislodging a sharp piece of stone. It gleamed in the noonday sunlight. He reached and picked it up, turned it over in his hand and saw, to his astonishment, that he was holding an Indian arrowhead. A very old Indian arrowhead.

Elizabeth Grosh and Mary Tennis had climbed the hand-hewn wooden ladder to the hay loft in Sammy Funk's barn. They had dragged Peggy Ann and Cynthia Sue, two well-worn rag dolls up the steep incline and settled into the stale stalks of straw to gaze out the high window at the expansive farm land beyond. It was a good day to be alive, young, and unconcerned with the troubles of a world better left to adults, or at least, to older brothers. They both knew their lives were about to change yet again, but this time, on a more stable footing, to a permanent circumstance they might once again call home.

"Do you like boys?" asked Mary. The girls, both eleven years of age, had bonded since arriving in Illinois and discussed such matters of importance at regular intervals. The dolls listened quietly and respectfully, keeping their own opinions to themselves.

"Boys? Ugh. I have four older brothers, you know," was Elizabeth's curt answer.

"Well I have a brother too, dummy. But I don't mean *brothers*, I mean *boys*."

"Oh, I don't know. They're OK, I guess."

"Aren't you going to get married someday?"

"Are you?"

"I've already decided that," answered Mary. "I'm going to marry one of your brothers."

"You are not!"

"I am. I talked it over with my sister Cathy. She's going to marry your brother Will and I'll marry one of the others."

"Which one? Philip...he' s the oldest. He'd be a good husband for you."

"Oh no, he's too old. It would be like marrying my father."

"Girls can't marry their fathers, you know."

"Why not?'

"'Cause they're already married, silly. Well, then there's John or James. James is more your age."

"Well, I like them both, but James is kind of immature, don't you think? I'd have to wait for him to grow up."

"What do you mean, immature?" came a voice from behind the girls. They turned and Mary flushed crimson as she saw a face peeking over the edge of the loft. There, balanced precariously on the ladder was Elizabeth's brother, James.

"How long have you..."

"Long enough!" James hoisted himself up into the hay loft and joined the girls at the window. "Hey, look down there! There's a grand pile of hay below. Bet you we could jump into that."

"No, James!" cried Elizabeth. That's too dangerous."

"Oh come on. Are you chicken? I'll go first, but you have to promise you'll jump too. Watch this!" James grabbed the two dolls, Peggy Ann and Cynthia Sue and sent them plummeting toward the hay stack below.

Mary stood, eased up to the edge of the window and looked down. It didn't seem *that* far. Elizabeth clutched at the girl and cried, "No, Mary! Don't. Don't be foolish—just because James is such an idiot!" But she began to lean outward and Elizabeth became afraid she wouldn't be able to hold her back. Just then, a new voice resounded across the hay loft.

"Elizabeth! Mary! James! What are you doing up here. Don't you know it is dangerous? Come down immediately!" The imposing figure of John Grosh stood on the ladder. Mary, startled by his booming voice, would have jumped out into space had not Elizabeth pulled her back into the loft. The three children turned, looking sheepishly at the older boy, then slowly, but dutifully, made their way back toward the ladder.

As they exited the barn and ran to the hay stack to

rescue their dolls, the girls looked at each other with sagacious and canny smiles. "I know which one I'll marry," said Mary Tennis. "It's going to be John."

CHAPTER 29
THE PRAIRIE PIRATES

Oregon, Illinois, 9 September, 1846

Philip, John, Will, and James waited at the counter of Scott's Hardware Store in the town of Oregon while the clerk checked on their order. It was an extravagance, but a well deserved one: a Phoenix Stove Works cast iron cook stove made by the Comstock Company in Quincy, Illinois, and shipped up the Rock River to Oregon. Well, Father had his John Deere plow, why shouldn't Mother have a decent stove to cook on? The boys had pooled what little money they had saved and father Isaac had added enough to pay the $42.25 for the "Golden Economy" model with the nickel-chromed door pedal attachment and the portable outside oven shelf. It wasn't her birthday, or anything like that. It was just the finishing touch that the log house needed and the kind of present they hoped would let their mother know how much they loved and appreciated her. Especially with the baby coming soon.

The cabin building had gone smoothly. Isaac's land purchase of 160 acres had included 40 of timber. They had felled tall pines and dragged them to a high, level spot. There they built a log framed building in the German style called Fachwerke. They peeled the logs of bark and squared them, then cut them to length and notched them near the ends so that they could be laid over one another making a secure lock joint at the corners. Gaps or spaces between logs they filled with rock and plastered over, inside and out. Come spring they could cover the exterior with siding.

They split logs and planed boards for the floor and a ceiling where they constructed a sleeping loft. The sleeping loft was reached by a ladder made from spruce saplings. Beds were bunks attached to the outside walls with curtains hung to afford privacy. As they had in Pennsylvania, Isaac and Catherine slept downstairs where the large open room was used as a kitchen, dining room, living room and bedroom.

The door and windows were simply rectangular holes cut into the walls as the logs were being placed on top of each other. The holes were framed and fitted with mullioned windows. There was no glass available for window panes so oiled paper was used instead. This let in the light—and the cold. The door was a heavy, solid slab of squared logs.

They built a fireplace and chimney from some of the larger stones they had removed from the land. It was in this fireplace that Catherine had been cooking, setting an iron pot with legs over the burning embers. The new Phoenix stove had an oven she would now be able to use for pies and roasts and to bake bread. And Isaac would be able to move his rocking chair in front of the fireplace when winter came.

There was a good spring along side of the cabin providing fresh water. And several yards away, the boys had dug a deep hole for a privy. The outhouse erected on top of this was a two-seater, a necessity for a large family such as Isaac's. A small shed soon joined the house and there were plans for a barn and a corral for animals. Although the winter was approaching, Catherine had staked out a plot for her garden and had begun cultivating the earth. In the spring she would plant flowers as well as vegetables— flowers like snap dragons and daisies that reminded her of home.

So today, the boys had brought a horse and wagon, borrowed from Sammy Funk, to the town of Oregon on the Rock River to pick up the new stove. As they waited at the hardware store, a commotion outside caught their attention. Cries of "They're acquitted!" and "They're freed!" came from a crowd milling about in the street. Curious, they watched through the store's plate glass window as a number of men were hoisted upon the shoulders of others and carried across the town square amongst the cheering multitudes. The store clerk returned, saying that he had sent a boy over to the warehouse to bring up the stove on a dolly.

"What's going on out there?" asked John.

"It's the trial of the Regulators. They're acquitted," answered the clerk.

"Regulators on trial? That seems strange," offered Philip.

"Kind of took the law into their own hands, they did. What other law there was is a good question, though."

"I see. What exactly did they do...I mean, what were they supposed to have done?"

"You've heard of the 'Prairie Pirates,' haven't you?"

"We've heard of river pirates," said James. "Met some of 'em, too!"

"There has been a big band of robbers in this county for years and years. Mostly horse thieves. Steal that and anything you didn't tie down or set a mean dog to guard," continued the store clerk, pulling up on a pair of dark green suspenders that were doing a poor job of holding his pants above his hips. "They've been well organized. Have stations where people let them hide their stolen goods as they pass it along."

"Kind of like an Underground Railroad for bandits!" said Philip.

"Yes, exactly like that. The ring leaders, the Driscolls, the Brodies, Aikens, they controlled it all. They'd steal, they'd pass counterfeit money, they'd even murder when people tried to stand up to them. If they got caught and went to trial you could bet there'd be a pirate on the jury. They'd get off!

"One time—you know, Oregon here is the county seat—well, we were building a new courthouse. Almost finished and some of the pirates, half dozen or so, were in jail. The other pirates, they figured they'd spring 'em and destroy all the evidence so they set fire to the courthouse. Burned it down. Only the jail didn't burn. Three of them pirates did get sentenced, but the rest got off."

"Sounds like a bad situation for law abiding folks."

"Well, some people got together and swore to bring the Prairie Pirates to justice. One way or the other. Got to be almost two hundred of them in time. Called themselves the Regulators.

"One of the leaders of the Regulators, a John Campbell, started getting threats from one of the Driscolls. Threats of murder. One night, he went outside his house—which people never did without carrying a rifle or a pistol. But he didn't see old man Driscoll and his son hiding in the bushes. They rose up and shot him dead as a doornail. Fell down right in front of his wife, the poor lady.

"People were outraged and the Regulators, they finally rounded up the Driscolls. Put 'em on trial and the Regulators themselves, a hundred and eleven of 'em, sat as the jury. Of course they found them guilty and sentenced them to hang. Only the Driscolls, they asked to be shot, humane like."

"That certainly sounds like a better way to go."

"Yes, well the Regulators formed themselves into two long lines and one Driscoll got 56 bullets in his body and other one, 55. Easy numbers to remember—it made such a sweet racket! Others of the gang were rounded up but there's still many a Prairie Pirate out there."

"So then the Regulators were arrested?"

"John Jenkins was the new leader. He and the others were indicted and the trial... we feared the worse as the pirates still have some influence. But it appears from all the shoutin' that justice is done. The Driscolls was hated by honest folk and that Campbell feller that they murdered was much admired for his efforts in bringin' peace and the law to Ogle County."

The boy returned reporting that he had pushed the dolly with the new stove out in front of the hardware store. The boys paid for it and went outside to load it on the wagon. There it was in all its glory: shiny chrome trim, enameled top and intricate designs mmolded into the cast iron body. The clerk appeared carrying a length of stove pipe and the six of them heaved and hefted and managed to lift the heavy stove onto the wagon which promptly sagged on its springs.

"Let's go watch the celebration," said James, pointing to the crowd in the square where an impromptu brass band had assembled and was making a dreadfully discordant noise. They strolled up the block to drink in the energy emanating from throng. There were farmers like themselves, store keepers, mothers with children in tow and of course, representatives of the Regulators who were back slapped or bear hugged and enthusiastically cheered. "Law and order!" "Justice prevails!" "Up the Regulators!" were the cries. It appeared that a turning point had been reached in the county where predatory bandits would no longer remain unpunished or cause good men and women to fear to venture out at night.

The Grosh boys added their congratulations to the informal celebration, meeting some of the Regulators including their leader, John Jenkins. They turned to go back to the wagon but when they reached Scott's store, the street was empty. Someone had stolen the horse, wagon and their new stove! For a moment they stood in disbelief. Then feelings of foolishness, guilt and anger compounded and they looked at each other with trepidation.

"What do we do now?" asked Will.

"We've got pirates? We need Regulators," said Philip. He hustled his brothers back to the square where they sought out the man who had been introduced to them as John Jenkins. Explaining their plight simultaneously with four uncoordinated voices, the boys got Jenkins' attention, if not his understanding.

"Woe, slow down. One at a time," said the Regulator.

"Somebody just stole our horse and wagon," said Philip. "Had to have been just a few minutes ago."

"Then there's no time to lose," replied Jenkins, and motioning the boys to follow, led them to a horse and buggy parked nearby. Into this they all piled and Jenkins asked, "Which way?"

"Well, it was pointed in that direction—out of town."

The lighter buggy and fresher, younger horse was faster than the wagon with its heavy load of iron stove and soon they caught sight of a cloud of dust on the road ahead. As they neared the wagon, Jenkins whipped his horse and the buggy shot ahead. He passed the wagon and stopped in the middle of the road, blocking the wagon's progress. Raising a hand he ordered, "Stop!" The wagon came to a halt. There were two men in it.

Philip, John, Will, and James jumped out of the buggy and ran up to their wagon.

"What do you want?" asked one of the thieves.

"That's our wagon and our stove," said Philip, clinching his fists.

"Oh ya?" said the man. "I think it's mine now." The man reached down and pulled up a rifle which he aimed squarely at Philip. For a moment, there was an impasse during which the two adversaries simply stared at each other, each hoping, no doubt, that the other would back down. Back in the buggy, Jenkins slowly moved his hand under the seat where he kept a rifle of his own. He knew he would be too late if the pirate decided to fire first. As the tension thickened, the pirate began to smile, his dirty teeth accenting the cruelty of his expression.

Suddenly, James leaped forward and grabbed the gun from the man's hands, the motion nearly unseating him from the wagon. Philip finished the job, taking advantage of the fact that the man was off balance, and pulled him down into the dirt of the road. The second pirate started moving toward the boys in spite of being out-numbered. Perhaps it was rage, perhaps stupidity, but on he came. By the time the man had jumped down to engage in the fight, Jenkins had arrived with rifle cocked.

After Jenkins had corralled the two pirates into the buggy and secured them with some rope, he turned to James and said, "That was a might fool-hearty thing you did, grabbing that rifle!"

"Well, you see, I recognized that gun as my papa's musket that we had thrown into the wagon this morning. That thing hasn't been loaded in a month of Sundays, 'cause it doesn't shoot straight. It probably would have exploded in his face, anyway, if it had had any dry powder in it."

Will reached down and picked the gun up from the dirt. He gave a quick perusal and shook his head. "James," he said, "I hate to tell you this, but this isn't Pop's musket. It's loaded and cocked and you're lucky to be alive!"

CHAPTER 30
PRAIRIE PIONEERS

Pine Creek Township, Ogle County, Illinois,
22 November, 1846

The first flakes of snow, a whisper of winter's promise, danced and darted in the shifting prairie winds. Some turned to watery dollops upon striking still warm rocks. Others stuck and lingered, coating the needles of tall pines and frosting the roof of the log house with an alien whiteness. The damp cold had not yet reached the bone chilling temperatures that would come, but stove and fireplace inside the dwelling were kept glowing with warmth for the house's newest occupant.

Baby Harriet was just over one month old. Back in Pennsylvania, her cousin, Silas Cornelius, had been born the same week. One day they would play together and attend the same white-washed school house that sat on a hill a mile up the road. For now, the school bell would summon only James, Mary Jane, Elizabeth and Emma to its single classroom, but the teacher, Katherine Bingaman, would attract the attention of one Philip Grosh.

Harriet lay in a wooden crib with hand-turned spindles that had been presented to Catherine and Isaac by Sammy Funk. Her eyes tried to focus on the spots of light that played across the wall as the wind rustled the paper window panes. Her mother hummed a soft tune as she gently tucked a quilted blanket around Harriet. The baby immediately kicked this off and expressed her displeasure with a series of cooing sounds and gurgles. Catherine laughed. Harriet cooed all the more.

The door flew open as the children returned from school. James dropped his slate and pencil box on the floor, incurring a harsh, "Pick it up and close that door!" from his mother. The girls climbed swiftly up the ladder to the sleeping loft where they had left their dolls engaged in a tea party, only to find that their younger sister, Katy, had modified the arrangement somewhat by tucking each doll under the bedclothes of her own bed, insisting that the "babies" were too young to drink tea and needed to take their naps.

The children had adjusted well to life on the Illinois prairie. It wasn't so different from their lives back in Huntingdon County, Pennsylvania. There were new faces at school, of course. There was that Josh Bomberger who kept teasing Elizabeth. Mary Jane teased her also, telling her she thought Josh was handsome, but this only made Elizabeth angry. Boys! There were enough of those at home!

James thought he was too old to still be in school. He should be out hunting with Philip and John. The two eldest boys did bring home prairie chickens, wild duck and the occasional rabbit. Now that the Grosh family possessed two more than adequate rifled muskets, (one procured from the river pirates and the other from the prairie pirates), it seemed logical to James that the hunting party should number three: the third weapon would be father Isaac's old musket.

Yesterday Philip and John had come upon a stag standing on a high rise near the pine woods. It was a beautiful animal, five points on each side of its antlers and nearly four feet high at the shoulder. Its grayish brown coat shimmered as steam evaporated in the crisp cold November air. They crept up on it quietly but the deer startled and sprinted into a stand of white pine, its white tail bobbing. The boys followed. They came upon it at the stream, its legs splayed as it bent to drink. The wind no longer at their backs, this time the boys approached undetected.

Both rifles raised to their shoulders, the boys looked each other, soliciting approval. Philip nodded and lowered his weapon, a silent answer to the question, "You or me?" John steadied himself and drew a bead on the animal's neck. "I'm sorry," he said to the deer in his mind. "You will give us sustenance for weeks and for this we thank you." His prayerful inner thoughts complete, he pulled the trigger. The stag collapsed.

They field dressed the deer and carried its considerable bulk home where they hung the carcass inside the small shed behind the log house. It would keep in the cold and there was plenty of time to butcher it into usable portions. Outside, the meager snow flurries failed to obliterate the blood trail between the stream bed and the log house. This was unfortunate as there were predators in the area that would be attracted by the scent of freshly killed white tail deer.

Today Isaac, Philip, John and William had continued clearing the land, hauling rocks and cutting trees. It was hard, time consuming-work. The top land was partially forested but the south sections were more like the treeless tall grass prairie over which they had traveled and needed only to be turned over by plowing. Their focus for this season was to expose as much of the rich loam of the virgin land as possible before winter.

"Getting darker earlier," commented Will.

"Winter's coming all right. We'll need a team to uproot some of these stumps," said John.

"Next spring we'll get more animals," said his father. "We've done well this fall. The ground will be frozen soon. Come spring we'll take that new plow to the land, turn this soil over. Plant. Then you'll see the bounty we can bring forth. True hard work is rewarded with abundant blessings."

"Well, I've got abundant calluses," said Philip.

As darkness thickened toward night they returned to the log house. The aroma of venison stew revitalized the weary men. Some cold cider quenched their thirst. Mary Jane, Elizabeth and Emma set the log table with Catherine's china plates, brought so carefully along the rivers and across the prairie without a single chip or crack. Isaac said grace and the meal was served in the flickering light of fire and lantern.

"Plain living, plain dressing and plain habits," said Isaac, "these are the principles by which we live."

"Ah," said Will, "but this food is not plain. It's delicious!"

"Thank you for saying so, Will," said his mother, "but

listen to what your father has to say."

"It is my desire," continued Isaac, "that you all keep to the teaching of our church and remember that family and community are important to a healthy society. There is much injustice in this country. There is greed and hatred enough to bring upon us the apocalypse! That's why we must live true to our values and be at peace with our fellow men."

"And women," said Catherine.

"And especially our women," agreed Isaac.

The children sat thoughtfully at the table, trying not to surrender to their natural tendency to gobble. Keeping plain habits, their father had reminded them, was paramount to leading the life of a Brethren family. But when the stew smelled and tasted so good...

"Father," began Philip, "I know it is the custom for children to remain a home at least until they reach twenty-one."

"Yes, Philip, that is true. But you will remember, I gave you older boys a choice when we discussed leaving German Valley."

"I know, Father, and I have wavered more than once when it comes to this tradition."

"Tradition it may be, but it is your desire that concerns me. Are you once again feeling the need to strike out on your own?"

"Not to strike out as such. But I've been thinking that I might be interested in becoming a teacher," said Philip.

"Ha!" laughed James. "You're interested in teaching, all right. In *the teacher*, that is."

"James!" scolded Catherine. "Don't taunt your brother."

"Oh, it's all right, Mother," said Philip. "He thinks I like his teacher, Miss Bingaman."

"And do you?"

"Well...she may not like me. I don't know. But it's beside the point. There is a seminary at Mount Morris where I could study. Learn to be a teacher."

"That's a Methodist seminary, Philip," said his father. "I don't know about their values."

"At least they aren't beholding to the Pope. They're protestant."

"They baptize babies," added James, meddlesome as usual. Brethren were only baptized once they became adults, able to make their own decisions, The silence that followed made it apparent that the discussion had concluded. The rest of the children, try as they might to emulate proper behavior, began to gobble.

Later, as James and Will sat at the checkerboard and the family was out of earshot, James said, "So what did you think of that?"

"Shh! They'll hear you, " said Will.

"No, really. What did you think of that?" James repeated, his voice now a whisper.

"Oh, I think Philip has always been out in front for us. Taking the first steps that we can't take. If he wants to be a teacher, I say, fine. He'll be a great one."

"No, I mean about staying on the farm until we're twenty-one."

"Oh, that. Well, what do you think?"

"I think that's a long time."

"Maybe for you, it is."

"And if Mom keeps having girls, we could be here for a really, really long time!"

The temperature began to drop during the night and a storm blew in from the north, bringing snow that heaped up upon the ground and drifted until it would reach the pioneers' knees in the morning. One of the wolves that had followed the deer blood scent to the shed stood staring at the closed door. The other wolves wandered restlessly around and around the small building, looking for a way inside where they smelled a great feast. The wolf considered the door: he'd seen this kind of thing before and not so long ago. It could be opened by the two-legs with no more effort than if a wolf might claw at it like...

Light streamed out from the lantern John held high as he opened the log house door. "Who's out there?" he called. There was a commotion as the wolf pack gathered to consolidate its strength in confronting this new unknown. John heard it, then saw six pairs of yellow eyes reflected in the lantern light. "Wolves!" he cried as he slammed shut the door. He retrieved his musket from the rack where it hung and began a frantic effort to load powder and ball. When finally he again threw open the door the pack had disappeared into the black night, their footprints obliterated by the falling snow.

Isaac and Catherine lay in bed covered by a feather-filled comforter. Baby Harriet, who had been fussing, lay between them. Catherine looked into Isaac's grey eyes and smiled.

"She's adorable, don't you think?" she asked.

"Of course she is. She'll be the prettiest and the sweetest of all our girls, I think."

"You really wished for another boy, didn't you, Isaac?"

"Oh, Cat, I don't know. I love our girls, but, the farm, the future of the Grosh line..."

"You have four boys now, Isaac. You should be proud. They'll all carry on for you. You know that."

"Could we not try one more time for a boy, Cat?"

"Not tonight, Isaac, dear. Not tonight."

The next morning was a Sunday. Isaac and his clan trudged though wind blown drifts, following wagon and carriage tracks, the only affirmation of a byway through the deep snow. The meeting house that served the Brethren as church was nearly a mile away. They had left Elizabeth to tend Harriet and Emma to entertain Katy while they braved the penetrating chill and pallid emptiness of the early prairie winter. Finally, they entered the building, shook the snow off their coats and sat down, occupying an entire row of seats.

As Isaac sat in the hard wooden chair his thoughts wandered. Did he have doubts about this new life? He didn't think so, yet the advent of winter curtailing his preparation of the land worried him. They were starting with nothing but an unbridled optimism, a belief that zealous enterprise would see them through. Hard work, plain living, the support of the community, family—these gave him confidence, energized him, spawned the vision of a bountiful new life.

Next to him, Catherine mused upon her own estimate of the future. Just as Isaac was driven to create and build,

Catherine was dedicated to maintain and nurture. She knew that the boys would eventually leave to start their own lives and the girls—she hoped this new world they had settled into would provide them opportunities, which for women in the nineteenth century meant marriage and children. The county was so sparsely populated! But it was growing. More and more came from Pennsylvania, Maryland, Ohio and Indiana everyday. She hoped her sister, Amelia, and her family would make the journey soon. Dick Cornelius had returned to the east after obtaining an option on a farm in Mount Morris. But Amelia, who the Grosh children called "Aunt Polly," wasn't eager to uproot her family. Catherine thought how different her life would be had she opposed Isaac as her sister had opposed her own husband. But that wasn't her nature.

Philip couldn't help looking at Katherine Bingaman who sat with her mother and father a few rows ahead of him. There was something about the way those thick curls of auburn hair fell across the nape of her neck. Was his sudden interest in becoming a teacher due solely to his fascination with this young woman? He would have to give it much thought. His plan for an advanced education was a laudable one, a chance to help other people. It didn't hurt that the object of his admirations was also so inclined.

And John. John was the dutiful son, a reality he pondered as the church meeting progressed from hymns to quiet mediation. He loved working with his father and took to farming with a passion he hadn't anticipated. And yet... and yet there was a glimmer of restlessness in his soul. Perhaps a spark of that wanderlust that had possessed Isaac had infected him, kindled by the great journey they had recently undertaken, leaving him with a sense of something incomplete and unfinished.

William's eyes were fixed upon Cathy Tennis. He was of an age when the future was merely a word bandied about by other people, people unsettled in the present. His present was more than adequate: it was intriguing. He loved the new land, the prospect of farming it, raising animals, getting to know his neighbors. Some neighbors more than others. When she caught his glance and smiled he realized he was grinning idiotically and he blushed. Yes, the present was full of potential for William.

James, on the other hand, was still fixating on the relentless years of drudgery and boredom he saw as his future. There was nothing to do here in Pine Creek. Had he been older he might have joined the army to fight in the Mexican war that President Polk had initiated. His was an awkward age, fraught with the frustrations of adolescent discontent, anxiety, ennui. He had excess energy but little ambition, especially when it came to knuckling down and contributing selfless, arduous sweat. He was immature, it was true, but he loved his family.

Mary Jane had always been something of a tomboy, preferring the company of her brother, James, with his antics and adventures to that of her sisters and their friends with their dolls and domesticity. Now, though, she felt a change drawing near. Something was stirring within her that both puzzled and excited her. Something as yet undefined but propitious, like the first fragrant breezes of spring—so dazzlingly incongruous now that winter had arrived. There was a boy, Peter Avery, at her school. Not that she liked him, for who could care a whit about boys? But his older brother who came to walk him home after school...

The snow had stopped but the wind blew it up against the log house and slapped it against the windows. Elizabeth was rocking Harriet in her father's rocking chair, its runners creaking against the soft wood flooring. A log she had just put in the fireplace cracked loudly, its sap not dry. Emma and Katy played with dolls on the braided rug in front of the fire. Emma suddenly jumped up, inspired with an idea.

"I'm going to take Katy outside and build a snowman," she said.

"You stay by the house," Elizabeth warned. "John saw wolves outside last night."

"Oh, we'll be careful. Come on, Katy, lets get our coats on."

She had to push hard to move the snow that had piled up against the door. The cold was invigorating after the radiance of the fire and the stuffiness of the house. The girls ran and jumped into snow drifts and laughed the laughter of the young who live so solidly in the present that fear or worry never affects them. They made snowballs with mittened hands, ice crystals sticking to knitted wool. These they rolled across the snow to make the snowman's body. The morning sun was low in the sky, casting long shadows from the few remaining trees on the property. Another long shadow, one with four spindly looking legs stretched out from the tree. Katy saw it first and stopped working on the snowman to stare at the strange apparition that seemed itself to be made of snow.

The wolf inched its way toward the girls. Emma still hadn't noticed it. Overhead, a large black crow winged its way across the gray sky, cawing as if to warn the humans of impending peril. Emma turned and saw the wolf crouched down and crawling toward them through the snow. She drew Katy to her and encompassed her in her arms. "Shoo! Go away," she shouted. But still the wolf moved forward.

Emma, clutching Katy, backed up to the door of the log house and reached to pull on its heavy bulk. It wouldn't budge. Still the wolf came closer. She imagined it springing into the air and leaping upon them, its fangs sinking into the flesh of their necks. It stood on long legs and strutted up to within a foot of Emma and Katy, jaws open and dripping saliva, eyes staring without wavering into Emma's. The wolf shook himself and snow that had clung to his fur flew in all directions. It was then that Emma saw the jagged silver mark on its forehead that looked like a bolt of lightning. The mark that had given Emma the idea for his name.

"Lancelot!" she cried. "It's you!" The wolf raised his head to Emma's and licked her face with a hot, wet tongue. He looked at her for a moment, then turned and loped off across the snow and then was gone.

EPILOQUE

The farming community in Ogle County, Illinois grew as more and more people from Pennsylvania and Maryland joined their friends and families on the rich, fertile, virgin prairie. Isaac stayed on his farm in Pine Creek Township for all but three years of the rest of his life. The decade following his arrival there must have been one of constant loss, for while his farm flourished, his family began to leave him, one by one. Philip married Katherine Bingaman in 1849 and later became a teacher. He moved to the newly established town of Lanark, not a great distance away, but a separation in life style that no longer involved him in Isaac's daily reality.

David Roland, was born to Isaac and Catherine in 1850, a son at last—after a succession of five daughters. Dick Cornelius, back in Pennsylvania again, married Sara, his childhood sweetheart. Catherine never got to see her sister, Amelia, again for the Cornelius family hadn't moved to Illinois by the time Catherine died in 1851, leaving Isaac devastated and lonely, with a new baby to raise. He plunged not into despair, but into the development of the farm, increasing the size of the house and adding buildings to house the farm laborers that came to work for him. There may even have been a hidden room, a link in the Underground Railroad, as the Fugitive Slave Act passed in 1850 stated that runaways must be returned to their owners, and the prairie pioneers would certainly have resisted it.

William left the farm in 1850 when he turned 21. He married Catherine Tennis, in 1852. Like his brother, Philip, he opted for a non-farming profession, becoming apprenticed to a shoemaker, then working for the Illinois Central Railroad, then briefly returning to farming, renting a farm in nearby Buffalo Township. But again he reinvented himself, moved to Dresden, Iowa, and worked there as a druggist.

John and James left Illinois in 1852 for California and the gold rush (but that's another story). John didn't return until 1860 but then married Mary Jane Tennis and bought his own farm, just up the road from Isaac's. His farm consisted of 240 acres, even larger than Isaac's. It featured a number of fresh springs and a large pond where John's children would fish and swim in the summer, and ice skate when it froze solid in winter.

The daughters all married, except for Harriet, who died in 1859 at the age of thirteen from scarlet fever. Mary Jane married Charles Ayres in 1854. Elizabeth married Joshiah Bomberger in 1855. Emma stayed at home until 1860 when she married John Arnold and made a home in Mount Morris. Katy married Jesse Palmatier in 1863, the last of the children to leave home.

My Great Great Grandfather, Isaac, was a lonely man during those years. He did remarry, in 1868, to a young widow, Catherine Lutz. Together they had one more child, Verna, in 1869. It brought the total of progeny for Isaac, counting those who died, to 12.

My Great Grandfather, John, and his wife, Mary Jane Tennis had three children: two girls, Ida May and Hattie Emma, and my Grandfather, Alexander, all born on the farm. Mary Jane died in 1870 and John remarried two years later, and had one more son, Otis. Alexander moved to Naperville, Illinois, nearer to Chicago, where he was mayor during the Depression years and ran a soup kitchen. My father was born there in an apartment over the butcher shop that Alex ran with another man.

NOTES ON THE STORY

This has been, first and foremost, a work of fiction. It was inspired by the history of my Great Great Grandfather, Isaac Grush, who brought his family from Western Pennsylvania to Illinois in the mid-nineteenth century. I've endeavored to present that story the way it *might have happened*, using what meager evidence I could ferret out of the somewhat muddled genealogical resources provided by the Internet and the few written records I uncovered.

A word about names: Our family name is Grush, not Grosh, (and may have been derived from the French, De Grush or De Gruchy) but I chose to name my characters after the more common German name, Grosh, for two reasons. It enabled me to distance myself a little from the characters while writing, although I still could not help but think of them as family, albeit, one I never met. Second, the Grush family sometimes appears in census records as Grosh, a circumstance no doubt the result of misreading of handwritten records, or an assumption by the record keepers that we were related to another family named Grosh (although there was no relationship), who immigrated from Germany to Lancaster County in Pennsylvania, about the same time as my ancestors.

I kept most other names without change, which may be confusing, as the story has so many characters with similar given names. There is Catherine, Katherine, Cathy, Katy, etc., and a couple of Mary Janes. But German naming tradition follows the pattern of calling the first born male after the father's father, the second after the mother's father, and so forth, thus there are multiples of Isaac, Philip, John, Catherine, Mary Jane and the others. To have changed them would have confused *me* even more.

So what do I know about my family? There is an old, slim pamphlet about the Grush family history written by

William Bomberger, the son of the Elizabeth of our story. In it he states that they "went to the Ohio river, not far from Pittsburgh, where they built a raft...drifted with the current, aided by pike poles...reached the great Mississippi River where they...hired a steamboat to pull them up to what is now Savannah, Illinois." I was intrigued but somewhat incredulous about this idea of drifting on a raft on the river when there are so many stories of pioneers traveling by wagon train. How was it possible? What was it like?

There are other short biographies and some obituaries that refer to that trip. Some say they traveled by raft and some say by boat. As I began to research the era of pioneer migration west from the states of Pennsylvania and Maryland, I learned that river travel was very common, and for people going to Ohio, Indiana or Illinois, probably more practical. Flatboats, keelboats and large rafts transported people, animals and goods along canals and the Ohio and Mississippi between places as far away as Philadelphia and New Orleans. The steamboat was gradually becoming more important (and expensive) and the railroads were still in their infancy.

But why schlep all your household goods over the mountains to Pittsburgh when the canal went right through your town? It made more sense to me that Isaac and his family would have built or bought a flatboat, a more common and safer way to travel, and then go by way of canal and inclined railway as I described in the story.

Phillip Eby, in his letter (both he and the letter are real, although the letter was addressed to his other uncle, William Grush, Isaac's brother), claims he went all the way home by water. The author, Charles Dickens, describes a similar voyage he took in 1842 in his *"American Notes,"* although he traveled by steamboat, not raft. Now someone will no doubt e-mail me with a nice scan of some old tin type showing Isaac and his family floating down the river on a *raft*, and I hope that happens. But for now, and to make the story more interesting, I'll vote for the flatboat theory.

Anyone writing a historical novel will run up against the "time-traveler's syndrome" wherein the most interesting events of their chosen epoch will be out of synch with the plot. It is quite tempting to alter times, places and even people to fit into the story more conveniently. For me, writing about the year 1846, I felt marooned in what I thought was an uneventful, even boring time frame: the Indian wars in the eastern United States were over and the American Civil War wouldn't begin for nearly a decade and a half. But then I looked more closely. I found some occurrences and locations along the route that spoke volumes about our country and the foibles and failings of its people.

There were only two or three spots in the text where I purposely violated time and place. The Tennis family, whose flatboat is linked to Isaac's, were actually in Indiana until after 1850. The strife concerning the "Prairie Pirates" happened earlier, about 1841. And the Atta Boy wasn't commissioned until much later. The pirates at Cave-In-Rock operated from the turn of the end of the 18th century to about the 1830s. The story of Billy Potts and Potts Inn is probably myth; in fact, an ancestor has penned an extensive and well documented rebuttal showing that there was no evidence the Potts ever killed anyone. Pirate bands did operate all over the area, however. Everything else of historical significance has been more or less accurately portrayed. For instance, Philip *could* have met Steven Foster or Mark Twain—at least I refrained from interjecting Abraham Lincoln into the story, although he *was* involved in the Blackhawk War and also took a flatboat down the Mississippi to New Orleans—twice. But again, much earlier than the years in which our story takes place.

There was a real Jacob Green, a runaway slave who, it is said, escaped over the Allegheny Inclined Railroad. The story he tells is based on a real story, related by another former slave. The story of Dan Rice among the Mormons, Rice being one of the most famous early circus clowns and very possibly the model for the well known image of "Uncle Sam," is also well documented and at least as true as any circus story can be expected to be.

The routes of the Underground Railway are unfortunately not as well documented as one would wish, but the places mentioned in the text existed, notably the cave system in St. Louis. The "Old Slave House" in Illinois was a testimony to the viciousness with which blacks were treated, even in the supposedly free state of Illinois. It makes sense to me that Isaac and his family would have helped a runaway slave. The Brethren were opposed to slavery and were also pacifists. This must have placed them in an awkward and conflicting position once the Civil War started.

Sammy Funk was a real person. The Funk family was wide spread in the region and one account of Isaac's arrival in Illinois claims he was met at Savanna by Sammy Funk. There is a question in my mind as to whether Isaac did buy his farm land from the government or whether he simply settled on it and made a claim as earlier pioneers may have done. One account says he bought 160 acres for $1.50 an acre. He did build a log cabin when he first arrived. The German building technique I described in the text would have been fairly elaborate, as many log houses were assembled by simply stacking up logs, bark and all, and filling in the cracks with whatever was at hand. Bomberger mentions that the windows were paper, and further states that he himself was born in the log cabin. He also writes about attacks by wolves.

A Partial Bibliography for Further Reading

Bodmer, Karl. *Maximilian, Prince of Wied's Travels in the Interior of North America, 1832–1834.*

Brown, Maria Ward. *The Life of Dan Rice by Maria Ward Brown.* Long Branch, N. J., 1901.

Calarco, Tom. *People of the Underground Railroad.* Greenwood Publishing Group.

Carr, William R. *Isaiah L. Potts and Polly Blue OF Potts Hill.* www.heritech.com/soil/genealogy/potts/uncle_isaiah.

Chapman,Charles M. *"Prairie Pirates (The Banditti)" from History of Pike County, 1880.*

Clarke. *The Biographical record of Ogle County, Illinois.* S.J. Clarke Publishing Company.

Clemens, Samuel (Mark Twain). *Life on the Mississippi.* James R. Osgood & Co., Boston, 1883.

Dickens, Charles. *American Notes for General Circulation.* published in England by Chapman & Hall, 1842.

Eby, Cecil. *"That Disgraceful Affair," The Black Hawk War.* New York: Norton, 1973.

Egle. *Egle's History of Huntingdon County, 1883.*

Ehle, John. *Trail of Tears: The Rise and Fall of the Cherokee Nation.* New York: Anchor Books.

Fedric, Frances. *Slave Life in Virginia and Kentucky; or, Fifty Years of Slavery in The Southern States of America.* London, Wertheim, Macintosh, and Hunt, 1863

Foste , J. Heron. *A Full Account of The Great Fire at Pittsburgh of the Tenth Day of April, 1845.* Pittsburgh: J. W. Cook, 1845.

Jahoda, Gloria. *Trail of Tears: The Story of the American Indian Removal 1813-1855.* Henry Holt & Co.

Kett, H.F. *The history of Ogle County, Illinois.* Kett, H.F. & Co. Chicago

Lansden, John M. *A History of The City of Cairo, Illinois.* R. R. Donnelley & Sons Company, Chicago, I910.

Milligan, Harold Vincent. *Stephen Collins Foster: a biography of America's folk-song composer.*

Musgrave, Jon. *Slaves, Salt, Sex & Mr. Crenshaw: The Real Story of the Old Slave House and America's Reverse Underground R.R.* Publisher: IllinoisHistory.com.

Rothert, Otto A. *The Outlaws of Cave-in-Rock.* 1923.

Rupp, Israel Daniel. *History of Lancaster County: To which is Prefixed a Brief Sketch of the History of Pennsylvania.* Gerlbert Hills Publisher, 1884.

Shurtleff, Mark. *Am I Not A Man? The Dred Scott Story.* Orem, UT: Valor Publishing Group.

Austin, Steward. *Twenty-Two Years a Slave, and Forty Years a Freeman.*

Utah Academic Library Consortium. *Trails of Hope: Overland Diaries and Letters, 1846–1869.*

Warren, William Penn. *"Ballad of Billie Potts."*

ABOUT THE AUTHOR

Byron Grush and his wife Martha live in Delavan, Wisconsin. He has been a filmmaker and teacher and is the author of a book on hand-drawn animation, *The Shoestring Animator*".

Made in the USA
San Bernardino, CA
03 December 2013